Gillian Eden-Walley is a retired concert pianist. Her early studies were with a pupil of Tobias Matthay and then at the Royal College of Music in London with Angus Morrison, Cyril Smith and Herbert Howells. After winning the Countess of Munster Award she settled in Devon, giving recitals, television and radio performances. Gillian Eden-Walley also established a reputation as a first-class piano teacher. She returned to England after two years abroad and settled in Berkshire, giving the occasional charity recital and enjoying her passion for the garden.

To Albert Fullbrook, an inspirational musician and devoted husband.

Gillian Eden-Walley

KEYS TO THE HEART

To Pam

Best wishes from

Gillian

xx

AUSTIN MACAULEY PUBLISHERS™

LONDON · CAMBRIDGE · NEW YORK · SHARJAH

A CIP catalogue record for this title is available from the British Library.

ISBN 9781398492851 (Paperback)
ISBN 9781398492868 (ePub-e-book)

www.austinmacauley.com

First Published 2023
Austin Macauley Publishers Ltd®
1 Canada Square
Canary Wharf
London
E14 5AA

Charlotte Wall for her computer expertise and editorial assistance. Also many thanks to my husband, Walter, and close friends for their support and encouragement.

Table of Contents

Prologue

It was a wet and windy day in early November. The autumn had been warm and sunny so the garden was still colourful. The fuchsias, asters, cyclamens, and roses were displaying their flowers with defiance, challenging the cold winter to come. The weeping beech presented its cascade of russet leaves but the Robinia had lost most of its golden foliage.

Violet viewed the plants and shrubs with a deep sense of satisfaction. Her horticultural journey had begun in Devon where the creation of a garden had been an unexpected pleasure. She had designed and planted the present one and although Violet disliked the chill and lack of activity during the winter, the autumnal colours and anticipation of spring bulbs cheered her spirits, nurturing her inner self. The Yuccas were displaying tall flower spikes and the bird bath was busy with splashing sparrows.

Rising late that morning, Violet had performed her morning ritual of lotions, potions and pills. There were repellents for unwanted garden inhabitants so why not for old age she pondered. The requirements of ageing included a healthy, but frugal, diet, so breakfast was brief and boring. The piano awaited her nimble fingers so the rest of the morning was devoted to Chopin and Beethoven.

'Are you ready for lunch?' her husband called.

'Yes, just my usual chicken noodle soup, please,' she replied. A treat of nuts and chocolate would follow with a mug of coffee.

Violet had recently compiled a scrapbook of her performing career. The memories had been a mixture of achievements and disappointments, as well as amazement at her behaviour at times. Her mother had reminded her on several occasions what a difficult person she was – clever but stubborn. A postcard that morning had stirred childhood memories. Violet had been considering writing a book for some time so she decided that afternoon to begin while her memory was still fortissimo. It would be partly biographical with family and friends assuming different names.

Part 1
Early Years

Chapter 1

The child sat in a high-chair while the grandmother attempted to feed her. 'You are not hungry again,' complained Granny. 'Stop playing with my brooch and focus on your food.' Grandma was not known for her patience but the shining brooch and lace blouse she wore were much more interesting to Violet than food.

'You will not grow into a strong, healthy girl unless you eat,' said Grandma. It was wartime in Europe and food rationing was in operation in England.

Starting in January 1940, dairy produce and meat were limited and in 1941 even clothes were rationed. Her mother managed regular meals for Violet, her sister, their half-sister and their father. Howard, their step-brother, was away fighting in Europe so there was a noticeable air of anxiety in the house. Her father equipped the air raid shelter with fancy lights and cushions, so eating there was like a picnic for Violet. The bombs starting falling on Plymouth in July 1940 with the Germans aiming for the naval dockyard.

They caused terrible damage, destroying twenty six schools, eight cinemas, forty one churches and two shopping centres. The housing casualties were appalling with loss of lives. One bomb fell less than a hundred yards from their house causing a large crater but fortunately no deaths. Violet had taken her favourite doll into the air raid shelter and held her close for comfort when she returned to the house. The blast of the bomb had blown out some of the windows so the decision was made to evacuate Violet, her sister and mother to an aunt and uncle who lived outside Budleigh Salterton. Aunt Emm was the sister of her father and the cottage was on an estate managed by her husband Frank. Joan, the step-sister, had the responsibility of looking after her father who was on duty with the Home Guard. She had just left school and was working in a local office doing routine jobs.

Life at Lilac Cottage was a relief for Violet's mother as Emm and Frank provided food and support. Violet was not aware of any family difficulties so enjoyed the country life with chickens and cows to watch, although she became a little nervous when the cows came close. She watched the rabbits racing across the nearby golf course and collected cones from the adjoining woods. Violet loved the walk through the woods with the smell of cones and moss. The only tearful moment was when her uncle hung the dead rabbits in the scullery and skinned them for rabbit pie. Years later when myxomatosis had eliminated so many rabbits, Violet still recalled the smell of rabbit pie at Lilac Cottage. The viral disease presented a problem to the authorities but the outbreak was allowed to run its course.

Aunt Emm was a superb cook and supplied cakes for the Women's Institute in addition to local celebrations. She had learned her skills from her mother and as Grandma was also living in the Cottage there were culinary treats every day. The cousins, Marie and Rose, tolerated Violet and her sister but they never became close friends.

The invasion of France by the Allies on 6th June 1944, known as D-Day, signalled the beginning of the end of the war so Violet, her sister and mother returned to Plymouth. The windows had been replaced, but food was still rationed and Violet still had to be tempted to eat at mealtimes. 'I'll put sixpence in your money box if you eat your vegetables,' said her mother.

'I ate mine but you haven't offered me any pocket money,' moaned her sister.

The first Christmas back at home had some extra presents. Usually, the girls had useful gifts like a new dressing gown or shoes but Violet craved a pram for her dolls. A second hand one had been repainted and she shouted with delight at seeing the green pram on Christmas morning.

Whenever Violet was not in the house, she was pushing the dolls' pram around the cul-de-sac. The neighbours were highly amused but thought it was very touching and that Violet would be a wonderful mother when she grew up.

With the war ending on the 8th May 1945, known as VE Day, street celebrations were organised and families looked forward to being united. Violet heard her mother answer the doorbell and wondered what news the telegraph boy had delivered. The memory of her mother's cry was forever connected to Howard's death. His vehicle had driven over a landmine and both Howard and his companion were killed instantly. The loss was devastating for the family.

Howard had been studying at Edinburgh University before signing-up to fight. With his good looks and intelligence, he was destined for a brilliant future. Violet's father never showed his feelings at the death of his beloved son, but with any wrong-doing in the family, his temper erupted. It was always short-lived but the girls and mother concealed many mishaps to avoid his rage.

Violet shared a bedroom with her sister, Donna. She had a gift for telling stories so they were often talking after "lights-out". Their father stormed into their bedroom on numerous occasions with a cane and struck their legs over the bedclothes. Violet eventually retrieved the cane and broke it in half, hiding the pieces under her mattress. On Mother's advice, there was no serious hunt for the cane or a replacement.

Joan had moved to live with a girlfriend so the spare bedroom was occupied by a lodger. The extra income paid for piano, ballet and elocution lessons as well as a few household extras. One lodger was a pompous bank clerk, who irritated Violet as he continually nagged her about eating enough food.

The doctor had examined Violet as her mother was worried about her lack of appetite and her thinness.

'Does she have coughs, colds or ailments of any kind?' asked the doctor.

'No,' replied her mother.

His final remark, 'Do you ever see a fat racehorse?' made her mother wonder whether Violet was destined to be a jockey and win the Derby. Violet subsequently told the lodger that she was a superb racehorse and could quite happily exist on cornflakes and bananas.

Family entertainment was provided by the radio and a record player. The regular programmes such as *Mrs Dale's Diary*, *The Archers and Housewives Choice* were never missed. Violet and her sister listened regularly to *Children's Hour*, *Dick Barton* and *Top of the Form*. Their parents enjoyed *Sunday half-hour* and *Grand Hotel Palm Court*

Orchestra on a Sunday evening while the girls finished their last minute homework for school the next day.

Violet and her sister would often visit their grandparents at the weekend. Grandma Nora was always entertaining as well as making the girls laugh. There was a dart board on the door in one of the downstairs rooms and the girls were given darts and shown how to score.

In the same room was full of bottles of spirits and wines. Their grandfather was manager of a large brewery and had an extensive alcohol store. On one occasion Nora gave a variety of drinks for the girls to taste. They only took small sips, but both Violet and Donna thought it very 'grown-up' giggling between the drinks.

Chapter 2

There was an upright piano in their front room and Violet showed an interest in learning to play at an early age. Funds were limited so her sister started lessons first. Donna hated practising and ended her tuition by refusing to go to lessons. Violet experienced her first piano lessons the same year she started school and it became apparent she had a gift.

Her grandmother was a brilliant pianist who could play any song she heard without requiring a copy of the music. 'Playing by ear' was a special gift that made her grandmother popular at parties or social gatherings. Most middle class homes had an upright piano so when she was a child Grandma Nora was invited to numerous celebrations.

Violet did not possess this ability but could memorise very quickly any piano score placed before her. She practised each morning before walking up the road to the Primary school with Donna.

The road was in a cul-de-sac so all the neighbours knew each other. Next door were a middle aged brother and sister. The sister was rather masculine in dress and appearance and years later Violet, during childhood reminiscences with a friend, commented that the sister might have been another man. No one would have even considered such a situation then as transgender and homosexuality were not discussed or even known about.

Violet was on friendly terms with them as they had two pekingese dogs that she adored. Adjoining their, semi-detached property was a family with two boys. The youngest, Russell, watched all the activities in the cul-de-sac, much to the neighbour's annoyance.

The older boy, Colin, would not have noticed if the house was on fire.

Violet tried for many years to attract his attention but he showed no interest in girls and to her amazement he became a policeman so she hoped his powers of observation had improved.

Another neighbour was Judy, who became a close friend of Violet. She was a year older but somewhat immature. Her father was very strict and very frugal so Judy had a second-hand pram as a baby, much to her mother's shame. Mrs Dean would have liked a large family which she was denied for financial reasons. Violet and Judith spent hours discussing the boys at school, dressing up in adult clothes and looking for sexual information in magazines.

The next door garden had numerous apple trees and the apples could be reached by climbing the wall adjoining the properties. Violet and her sister managed to steal a few without being caught. Then disaster struck when Violet slipped and sat on the spikes of the ladder holder. One spike penetrated her bottom.

'I think I have cut myself,' complained Violet. 'There is blood on my hand.' She started to cry so Donna rushed indoors to find their parents. A frantic rush to the hospital resulted in stitches to her bottom with the journey in the taxi necessitating numerous towels to stem the blood flow. Violet had felt no pain but took several days off from school.

'My pocket money has been stopped this month. I always end up being blamed for your accidents,' Donna complained to Violet.

The primary school times were years of achievement for Violet and she became top of the school. Her most important friend was Bella. They were inseparable with their friendship lasting well into adult life. Bella had a very well developed body that made her attractive to most of the boys. On one occasion it became 'Showtime' for the boys. A group would walk across to the park opposite to the school and on this particular afternoon the leader of the boys' group suggested a close look at Bella's chest.

'You show yours and we'll show ours,' he offered.

'No thanks, it wouldn't be worth the bother,' replied Bella.

'How about a shilling,' he said.

After much giggling, Bella revealed her large breasts. Violet was physically under-developed so her contribution was a quick display of rear cheeks. The display of male genitals was a distinct disappointment although the two girls had no previous experience to make a comparison.

There were damaged buildings in the area after World War II and the girls would be teased about ghosts walking in the ruins at night.

'I dare you to walk in there,' said one of the boys to Violet. It was early evening but almost dark so the ruins looked very frightening. She always hurried past them on her way home from a friend in the next road.

'Why don't you go into the buildings if you are so brave,' replied Violet.

'You can tell us then if there are any ghosts.' Violet ran past the boys into her cul-de-sac, afraid they might push her into the ruins.

The final year at primary school involved an examination, the eleven-plus. Although only nine years old Violet passed with high marks but she had to wait a year before attending a grammar school. She chose the one near to their house so she could practise the piano before walking to school with her sister. A financial advantage for the family was that Violet could wear the school uniform items that no longer fitted her sister. Clothing rationing was abolished in 1949 but the choice of material was limited. Their mother was an excellent seamstress and made most of the girls' clothes. They wore matching dresses, coats and had Sunday clothes for church. One of the neighbours commented that the girls looked like the Royal princesses.

The local piano teacher was not developing Violet's talent but he lived close to their house so Violet could walk to her lessons. She had very little sense of meal times due to her lack of interest in food and on one occasion arrived for her piano lesson an hour early before lunch instead of after lunch. The decision was made to arrange an audition with the best teacher in the West Country. Violet was told that the tuition would be more expensive.

'I can save my pocket money to pay for my music books and maybe have a lesson once a fortnight,' said Violet. She played two short piano solos to Henry, and to her delight was accepted as a pupil. The weekly lessons were arranged with the bill being paid in advance each term. Violet had met a man and musician who would transform her life.

Chapter 3

Once at the grammar school Violet became involved in sporting activities. She possessed excellent physical coordination and timing so became a member of the netball, hockey and tennis teams. Both parents were good tennis players and were members of a local tennis club where Violet and her sister practised on a disused court.

The piano lessons with Henry were the joy of her life. Violet started to win silver cups and medals at music festivals although she had to give up her hockey matches due to a damaged thumb on the morning of a concert.

Her performance at the Lord Mayor's Christmas Concert was a great honour for a 13 years old.

'I want a white dress with a red velvet ribbon around the waist,' said Violet to her mother.

'You need to be comfortable to play as well as long sleeves for warmth,' suggested her mother. Violet always felt the cold and later carried a hot water bottle in her music case to concerts.

The finished garment was a delight. The large bow of red velvet at the back with a full skirt of tulle and lace hung over the piano stool as she played.

Violet walked from the backstage room, where Henry had been waiting with her, to applause from a large audience. The piano lid was on half-stick so she had to wait while it was lifted to its full height. There were excellent press reports but the Headmistress at the grammar school was more interested in sporting achievements so there was no announcement during the morning assembly.

1953 saw sweets derationed so to satisfy her sweet tooth, Violet bought liquorice, humbugs, mint bullseyes and toffees with her remaining pocket money. Some of her pocket money contributed to buying new piano music. The most exciting event of 1953 was the coronation of Queen Elizabeth and the family visited a colleague of her father in Reading to watch the ceremony on television. They spent the day in front of the television eating sandwiches and cakes. There were endless cups of tea and their poor dog was not taken for his usual daily walk.

'Look, the Queen and the Duke of Edinburgh are leaving Buckingham Palace. Is that the Gold State Coach?' Violet was so excited about the Coronation that she had read all the Press and magazine articles. There was an annexe built outside the west entrance of Westminster Abbey.

It was glass fronted with models of the ten Queen's Beasts on the outside. Inside the Abbey there were carpets with a blue one in the nave, and the oak and beech chairs for the congregation were covered in velvet. Violet read about the richly embroidered robes of the clergy and the Archbishop of Canterbury who would crown the Queen.

'Her dress has been designed and made by Norman Hartnell. You know he is the dressmaker for the Royal family.

He designed her wedding dress as well,' stated Violet proudly.

An account of his task was published in one of the more expensive fashion magazines and Hartnell had made nine sketches for the Coronation dress. It finally had national emblems of the United Kingdom in addition to those of the Commonwealth embroidered on the white satin with jewels, sequins and beads.

'The Queen is going into St Edward's chapel to change crowns and wear the Royal Robe of purple velvet,' reported the BBC narrator. 'Her six maids of honour will carry the velvet train in the final procession to the waiting State coach.'

'The music is wonderful,' said Violet. 'I expect those choristers are very hungry and thirsty.' In fact it transpired that they had small sandwiches and barley sugar sweets hidden in their cassocks to keep them going during the long day.

The colleague had a holiday home in Cornwall where Violet and her sister spent a few weeks during the summer school holidays. The house had a pump for fresh water and only one fire in the living room. Violet and her sister slept in one large bed and experienced life on a farm. They collected eggs from the chicken hut and enjoyed drinking goat's milk for the first time, but Violet was horrified when the father killed a chicken by wringing its neck. She had a vivid picture for several nights causing nightmares.

They travelled by train as Father worked for the Great Western Railways and the family could travel cheaply. There were numerous trips to London and Violet experienced her first holiday abroad. It involved the ferry from Dover to Calais then a train to Paris.

'I feel sick,' said Donna.

'You do look a funny colour,' laughed Violet. Her sister did not realise she was suffering from sea-sickness, a lifelong problem for her when on a boat. 'I hope you are not going to spoil our trip to Paris,' complained Violet.

The French capital was a delight and Violet saw the Opera House for the first time in addition to all the famous buildings. She even managed to speak a few French words as the police refused to speak English to the tourists.

The second trip to France took the family to Nice. They saw where Somerset Maughan lived at Cap Ferrat and visited the Palace in Monaco, although Father had to wait outside the Palace as he was wearing shorts. Violet loved sitting outside a cafe watching the rich arrive at the Casino in their expensive cars. Drinking and eating outside a cafe was still a novelty.

Moving house was the next major event in the family. The bomb that had fallen near their home had left a crater and it was being cleared for new houses. One of them was going to be their new home.

It had a modern kitchen with a twin-tub washing machine instead of a copper lit by a coal fire. Previously Violet's mother would stir the clothes with wooden tongs to spread the washing powder, then lift the wet clothes into the sink before using the mangle to remove the water. Every Monday the house smelt of wet or drying clothes. The new kitchen transformed wash day. Father's ritual of lighting the fire disappeared as there was central heating, provided by the radiators so he missed the hours of prodding the coals and toasting the crumpets.

The girls had their own bedroom. Violet had organised hers with regards to her clothes and personal belongings but her sister's room was never tidy. 'Come and see my new bedroom,' said Violet to Bella, who was visiting to see all the new fittings.

'I have my own wardrobe and I am going to start a diary.'

Aunt Ruby, Violet's godmother, was visiting for tea. She thought the new house was so efficient.

'I wish we had central heating. George is very good at doing all the jobs around the house and garden but it is hard work for him.'

Ruby was married to George who had fallen in love with her when she was only 15 years old and still at school. She had wonderful long ginger hair.

Although already twenty five years old George waited for Ruby until she was of a marriageable age. He was devoted and brought her breakfast in bed every morning. Violet stayed with them when her mother had an operation in hospital but caught German measles that extended her stay for several weeks. Aunt Ruby took great care of Violet but she missed being at home and hated staying in bed away from the piano.

A year passed with music successes, sporting activities and schoolwork. Violet was still very thin but when she started her periods her weight increased slightly.

'You will need these towels when your period starts,' said her mother. No sexual implications were explained so Violet asked Bella. She considered her friend very advanced in bodily matters as she wore a brassiere.

'I think you can have a baby now but a boy has to inject something into you,' explained Bella.

'Do you get a strange sensation between your legs when you climb the rope in the gym?' asked Violet. 'It is like a sweet ache.'

'That is a sex spasm,' replied Bella. 'I heard my brother talking about something similar to his friend.'

Violet discussed and shared everything with Bella. They were both excellent at sport so played together in the netball and hockey teams as well as playing as the number one pair in tennis.

Henry took his pupils to regular orchestral concerts and Violet always sat next to him. He was rather amused at her reaction to many of the compositions. Violet heard Beethoven, Schubert and Wagner for the first time and tears often fell before the final chords. She met the well known conductor of the orchestra, a friend of Henry, and thought of the day she might be a soloist herself with the orchestra.

There were annual pupils' concerts in July and Violet gave her first public performance at the age of ten years. Her successes increased as well as her attachment to Henry. She had her piano lesson on a Saturday morning if there was no sports match. The weekend routine always included church on Sunday and after her confirmation Violet would go to the early Communion service. She then returned for Sunday school in the afternoon to play the hymns. She enjoyed the walk across the park to the church but there was an added attraction of the curate. Father Nigel was very handsome and most of the choir girls coveted his attention. He was very encouraging about Violet's musical future and after playing the hymns he drove Violet home in his Austin 7 on one occasion. Although she was delighted at the treat her heart was elsewhere.

Chapter 4

Violet gave her first solo recital in the church hall when she was 16 years old and the preparation was arduous. The previous year had begun with her having mumps. It was very painful as Violet had swellings in her stomach as well as her face. As soon as she had recovered there was an orchestral concert with Henry and some of the other pupils. It was an evening Violet would remember for the rest of her life.

'I'll run you home with the other pupils,' said Henry. Violet was the only one left as Henry drove into a lay-by. He put his arm around her shoulders and gently kissed her. The lingering kiss was something Violet had imagined for months.

'Are you worried by that?' asked Henry.

'No,' whispered Violet, 'I have wanted to do the same for some time.'

'I'll collect you from school tomorrow lunchtime,' Henry stated.

The meetings became routine. Henry played snooker most Saturday evenings at a club near Violet's grandparents' house. Violet had inherited Grandma Nora's musical talent, so it was not unusual for Violet to visit her. It was nerve-racking waiting outside the club but the joy of having an evening together overcame this. They often drove to the moors or somewhere they could look at the sea. At times Henry held her in blissful silence feeling satisfaction at just being close.

Henry always spent the Easter holiday in Bournemouth at an expensive hotel. There were concerts in the Winter Gardens and the week of luxury revived him from the teaching schedule. The first of many loving letters arrived from Bournemouth advising Violet about her recital programme. 'I am going to work in a hotel in Ostend. The owner is a friend of one of my aunts. Do you think I will make a good chamber maid?'

'I would like you to make my bed every morning,' said Henry laughing. Violet helped in the bar washing glasses as well as duties in the hotel rooms. She had a brief flirtation with a young Belgian scout and while he was attending the jamboree his parents took Violet sightseeing.

I have just seen & heard Arthur Rubenstein play at the Kursaal, she wrote to Henry. *He broke a piano string so we waited while it was replaced and then Rubenstein returned to finish the programme to loud applause & cheers. It was an amazing recital.*

A loving letter from Henry welcomed her home telling her what a fortunate pianist she was to have heard Rubenstein play.

The next event was a school trip to Austria.

'We will visit Salzburg, Mozart's home,' said Violet excitedly. 'My birthday is the same day as Mozart's, and his wife had the same name as my mother and my second name. Constanza is a continental version of Constance, so we have a connection and I will be playing more Mozart compositions when I return home.'

A visit to Hitler's retreat was included and also the idyllic White Horse Inn. Violet saw lakes and mountains for the first time, thrilling at the scenery. 'It must be wonderful to wake up and see all this every morning,' said Violet wistfully. 'But I wish the food was more appetising. I hate those German sausages and sauerkraut.'

Preparation for the solo recital was now Violet's main focus. The programme had been discussed with Henry with regular letters arriving for her. Apart from the music selection a piano had to be delivered to the church hall and also publicity arranged.

'You are not fully aware of the 'toil, sweat and tears' involved in a recital. The programme must display your versatility & technical ability to play the major classical repertoire,' wrote Henry.

Disaster struck just before the autumn term commenced. A neighbour had seen Violet with Henry on the moors and her parents discovered Violet's diary that contained details of their meetings. At 15 years, Violet was emotionally mature, as her piano playing revealed. She also possessed a stubbornness and tenacity that were surprising in one so young.

'We love each other and have done nothing wrong,' shouted Violet to her parents. 'He is essential for my future.'

A doctor stated that Violet was still sexually intact but Henry was horrified at the examination and professed a deep love for her.

The recital took up all her time and thoughts and a few lessons from Henry were allowed but it was decided to wait until the following spring for the solo recital. Another teacher was found for Violet but the traumatic event caused her to suffer a nervous breakdown whereby she constantly broke into tears. The recovery took several weeks but the piano provided an escape from the misery of not seeing Henry. Violet knew she was a gifted pianist but no one had told her how clever she was or recognised her intense emotions. To perform the Romantic repertoire of Chopin, Schumann and Liszt required an innate emotional response and understanding, and the love she felt for Henry enabled her to feel the passion in the piano music.

Violet had a quiet, reserved nature and disliked the normal teenage socialising but had accompanied her sister to weekly dances, hating every minute. At one dance, she met a young man who was on leave from the Navy. Peter became a regular boyfriend and Violet indulged his physical advances in an attempt to forget Henry. To improve her social life Violet accepted an invitation to a dance in the Dockyard, where she and her sister were entertained by officers from the Persian navy. It was a very elegant occasion so Violet wore one of her concert dresses.

She was performing at several concerts that winter with the most exciting one as guest artist with Vera Lynn.

The famous singer showed amazing kindness and generosity when she put her mink coat around Violet's shoulders to keep her warm while she was waiting in the wings of the theatre to play the piano. 'Have you seen the Press report?' Violet said excitedly. 'It says I was "musically the star of the evening" and "there is promise here of big achievements". It is all due to Henry's teaching.' Her parents refused to talk about lessons with Henry but Violet was not going to stop talking about him.

The grammar school gave more attention to sporting achievements so the press report about Violet was not mentioned by the Headmistress or the staff. Violet was made Head of one of the school's four houses and hers was St Monica. The post of Head girl was given to Bella when they reached the sixth form but Violet became her deputy later in the year. It was expected of Violet to take the entrance examination for Oxbridge, but her heart was set on the Royal College or Royal Academy of Music. She had been accepted at the Royal Academy two years earlier but her father thought she was too young to study in London on her own.

The Headmistress informed her that she would not be named on the Honours Board unless she went to university.

'You would think performing on the piano in public was disreputable,' complained Violet to Bella. 'There is no appreciation of my winning trophies at the Music Festivals. Surely, it is similar to winning a silver cup at one of the sporting events.'

Her solo recital was successful with an excellent press report praising her technique and musical ability. Henry appeared just before Violet started the first item and there was hostility between him and her parents. She felt nervous but Henry's presence gave her the confidence to perform the more difficult pieces. They still managed the occasional meeting but not in private. After passing the advanced Level examinations at school, Violet chose to work in the central library.

There was a developing music section run by a friend of Henry and Violet made a list of all the main music scores that should be available. She also performed at one of the concerts held in the Theatre of the Library in the presence of the Lord Mayor.

Henry came into the Library to see her and delivered one of his loving letters. Violet told Henry about her dates with Peter and that he was becoming quite serious about their relationship.

'You will attract many admirers, my darling, but you know my love for you is constant and for life. To think of anyone else loving you just hurts, of course, but you fill my mind and my heart.'

Violet was to inspire devotion and passion all her life but her two deep loves would be the piano and Henry.

Chapter 5

'Some news for everyone,' declared her mother one morning after breakfast. 'We are moving to Birmingham. Your father has been promoted so we need to start packing personal belongings in the next few weeks.'

Violet had thought about going to London regularly since the Royal Academy audition but to live anywhere else was devastating for her. She sent a letter to the post office for Henry immediately. His reply was heartbreaking but a treasure that Violet kept with her all her life. Their meeting that week was not possible so Henry wrote in detail his feelings and hopes.

How can I start this letter, darling? What terms of endearment not already used? I will just say 'my darling Violet' with a big accent on MY. At our final meeting I want you to have a memory of me (of us) that will bear every possible reflection. I am loving you so much, darling, all the time, brooding a lot, imagining so much, but overall looking for a way-out for both of us. Music and success must be the aim and not just an enjoyment of our love for each other. It only happens once, my darling, and this is the ONCE.

In retrospect, sweetheart, the past few years have been an experience full of such tender times and memories that we surely have enough to live on for a while.

Violet had to stop the tears falling on the pages, but she read on, choking back the sobs.

We have had some wonderful experiences, darling. The sound of the sea at Bigbury, the setting sun & moon coming up after – all these beautiful memories will be with me, darling, until memory is swallowed up in reality & we are together for good. As to your playing – the possibilities are immense. There is character and ability present in all you do, so my dearest girl, press on with it at all costs.

Henry made several references to their future and the new life in Birmingham that Violet was about to experience.

I can at least assure you that you will never be loved more deeply, sincerely and wholeheartedly than I love you now, my darling.

The letter ended with *all my thoughts are for you, my love is yours now & for always.*

On the train to Birmingham Violet repeated Henry's words to herself but the tearful journey seemed a nightmare to her. Her mind was working relentlessly how to get to London.

The family rented a house for a few weeks while their new home was being built but they hoped to move in before Christmas. Violet worked in the Central Library and Henry sent letters to her there. She used the poste restante at the main post office in Plymouth to tell Henry what was happening in Birmingham.

At least we can communicate, darling, wrote Violet. *I hate living here. The new house has all the conveniences, even a fireplace for Father to toast his crumpets, but the city is dirty and I have difficulty in understanding their speech at times because of the accent.*

'How about working in the Civil Service?' suggested her father. 'A good salary as well as a pension.'

Violet took the examination with a request to work in London.

'A letter has arrived from London,' called her mother. When Violet read she had passed the examination and was being offered a post in London, she fainted.

'What happened? Why am I lying on my bed?'

'You fainted, dear, when you read the letter from the Civil Service. We didn't know whether you had failed or you fainted with joy,' laughed her mother.

The months working in the Birmingham libraries had been tedious. No piano lessons and no Henry were making Violet miserable and depressed. She now thought of all the musical performances she could hear in London and she could contact Henry more easily. There had been a few letters at the library but not seeing or speaking to him left a constant ache.

'You will be back home in six months,' declared her father. 'London is not the exciting city you think it is.'

I am going to London, Henry!!! Violet wrote a joyful letter the following day to him. *You will be able to write to me without any subterfuge. I will try to come down to Devon before Christmas so let me know the best time, darling.*

Violet stayed with a school friend and visited her half-sister who was now married with two children. There had been no wedding celebrations as her father had disapproved of her future husband. It seemed no one was good enough for his daughters. The highlight of the trip was seeing Henry.

'London will be wonderful and the hostel is close to the Albert Hall, opposite Kensington gardens. Can you come to London for a day? We could enjoy a concert at the Festival Hall or Albert Hall,' said Violet, excitedly.

'I will try, my darling girl,' replied Henry, holding her close. 'It is 14 weeks since you left for Birmingham and to say you have been constantly in my mind is an understatement. You dominate my life and my thoughts, Violet. The separation has been agonising.'

Their meeting seemed very short but with the first kiss the magic returned to renew their deep love for each other. Henry's letter on her return to Birmingham reminded Violet of the film South Pacific. It was their special musical and he wrote the notes of 'Once You Have Found Her Never Let Her Go'.

'The reaction to our meeting has arrived, darling, and I feel a lot better in consequence. I was very nervous but feeling you physically beside me in the car dispelled all my nerves. To touch you after so many weeks was a pure joy and my daily prayer is that one day we shall be "as we hope".'

The letter mentioned the collapse of Donna's romance but how theirs was ever stronger and lasting.

Don't mind writing all your thoughts, dear little one, as I shall love to know them. Take all care of yourself, darling, and believe me, always YOURS, Henry.

Part 2
The Metropolis

Chapter 6

Violet stood on Westminster Bridge gazing at the Houses of Parliament, Big Ben and the Thames River. 'I am here at last,' she said to herself. 'I am free to enjoy music and see Henry.' Violet decided fate was with her.

She shared a room with five other girls. An arrangement that was good socially but had a few disadvantages. Three worked in the Civil Service, one was an assistant in an exclusive knitwear shop and the fifth was training to be a hairdresser in a well known salon. They became good friends and one of the Civil Servants, Sandra, had a Pakistan boyfriend who she hoped to marry. She was Scottish from a working class family and he, Ahmed, was from a wealthy family who had already chosen his future wife in Pakistan.

Sandra introduced Violet to his friends, some of whom worked in the Embassy and the others ran a travel agency. Babs often described the rich and famous customers that came into the knitwear shop in Picadilly. She spent her weekends with her Polish boyfriend who Violet never met. Marian, the training hairdresser had been a beauty queen in Wales and frequently returned from the salon with coloured hair. Violet always thought how stunning she looked and decided to do something interesting with her own hair. She had a head of tight curls which was not fashionable so a visit to a Kensington hairdresser resulted in shoulder length straight hair.

Violet loved the change in her appearance and wondered what Henry would think of the new look.

Violet settled into London life with enthusiasm. Her office was in Downing Street so she saw politicians and well-known visitors regularly. The Commonwealth Relations Office, or CRO, was validating the Duke of Edinburgh award in Parliament and Violet moved up from tea and post girl to personal assistant to a Principal. She was a kind and sympathetic woman who encouraged Violet to develop her career in the Civil Service, so Violet became involved in questions and matters being dealt with in the House of Commons. Mrs C, her boss, knew of Violet's passion for the piano and her gift for performing but also saw her potential as an executive in the CRO. Violet loved arriving at Westminster in the morning and hearing Big Ben strike nine o'clock, then returning to the hostel to read a letter from Henry.

There was a grand piano in the lounge that belonged to the Warden and Violet could play on it when there was no one there.

Having a monthly salary, enjoying a social life and shopping in Richmond were heavenly after Birmingham, but her heart yearned for the piano and Henry. She had regular letters from Henry and he suggested having lessons from one of the senior professors at the Royal College of Music, positioned behind the Albert Hall so within walking distance.

'You should be studying piano full-time at the Royal College,' said Angus.

'My father thinks a performing career is unreliable with no pension. My parents would agree to me becoming a music teacher as that is more respectable. But I want to perform,' replied Violet.

'Well, give some thought to studying at the Royal College as you have an exceptional talent.'

The months passed by with theatre visits, shopping in Oxford Street and ice-skating. Violet borrowed a pair of skates from one of the hostel girls and although her previous skill had been with roller skates she took to ice-skating quickly and expertly. Her other sporting activity was horse riding. Violet had lessons when she was living in Birmingham going to stables several miles from the city. To her amazement she eventually managed to stay on the horse when it jumped a three-bar gate. Her favourite place to ride was Richmond Park. It was the largest of London's Royal Parks and was created by Charles 1 as a deer park. Violet loved seeing the deer herd especially if there were young foals.

After one shopping expedition in Richmond the girls decided to wear their new clothes and pose in Kensington gardens for photographs.

Violet loved living in London with the well known buildings and experiencing all the activities that she enjoyed. The total freedom was heavenly for her.

The post was never read until all the girls returned from work in the evening. 'This one looks official,' said Sandra, handing a letter to Violet. Opening it with trepidation she read that the London City Council would be awarding her a grant to study at the Royal College of Music. Her shriek of excitement made the other girls jump.

'I am going to study the piano at last,' she cried.

'What about your job in the Civil Service?' enquired Sandra. 'You will have to give at least a month's notice.'

'I can start in January and leave my job at Christmas,' replied Violet optimistically.

There had been an interview arranged by Angus with the Principal of the Royal College. Her piano playing had been so highly recommended by him that Violet had been exempt from taking an entrance examination. She had been accepted for a four year performers course.

'I need a grant to pay for tuition and accommodation if I leave the Civil Service,' Violet told Angus. 'Perhaps the London County Council will provide some financial help.'

Violet was entitled to three years at a college or university and now to her delight the LCC agreed to provide a grant.

I'm going to study at the Royal College full-time! wrote Violet excitedly to Henry.

It is finally happening. I start in January and have decided to take violin as my second study.

Violet had only one worry and that was her age. She should have gone to a Music College at least eighteen months earlier. The letter from Henry cheered her mood.

If as we hope, you are now stepping on to the final stairs of the climb to fame. You have drive and ability. Develop the artistic side by "silent practice". THINK the music through, darling, and imagine all you want from it. I might even be permitted to congratulate you in the Artist's room! Whatever the course of events I shall always have you in my heart, both longing for your happiness and wishing you every success. Watching this from afar may well be my share, but I shall welcome all news of your progress.

Take care of yourself, my darling. All my love always, as ever.

Violet read it several times and put the letter in her music case. The need to feel his arms around her was very intense, so a trip to Devon before the term started was essential.

Mrs C was sorry, Violet was leaving the Civil Service but realised she was realising her dream of studying the piano. There was one special occasion that happened every November. Their offices were used for the Remembrance Day ceremony in Whitehall and Violet with her work colleagues had to clear the room for a member of the Royal family to watch the ceremony as their windows looked directly over the Cenotaph memorial. Once the Christmas break arrived Violet returned to Birmingham and informed her parents of her change of career. Both were amazed that Violet had organised a grant but were dismayed at her leaving the Civil Service.

'You will be without a decent income or pension. The life of a concert pianist is very precarious,' remarked her father.

She could feel the lack of enthusiasm and did not receive any praise for being accepted on a performers' course.

'I did not need to take the formal entrance examination,' Violet said proudly. 'The only problem will be paying for the hostel so I will need to find part-time jobs in the holidays. You thought I would only survive six months in London but now I am going to be studying for four years. You should be pleased.'

The Devon visit was arranged and Violet planned to stay with her uncle Reg and his wife Doris in their Great Western Railway tenant cottage. The temperature dropped to freezing in December and as there was only one fire in the living room, Violet's bedroom was very cold. Fortunately she had taken a hot water bottle with her. The visit had to include a Saturday so that she could meet Henry at the club in the evening. If he could see her on the Monday Violet was planning to stay longer and travel to Birmingham for Christmas.

There was anxiety and excitement at the meeting outside the club. Violet climbed into the Wolseley car without speaking.

'To the moors, I think,' said Henry. 'The sense of loss has been almost overpowering since you left Devon. We have seen each other only four times since your departure, darling – what a meagre ration!'

After they were parked in a quiet spot Henry held his arms to embrace her and Violet shed tears of joy and relief. His comment 'have faith in me and the future' would be her consolation during the following months. They managed a brief meeting overlooking the sea on the Monday.

'I miss the sound and smell the sea, it always seems to bring me comfort,' she told Henry.

The weather forecast gave snow in the Midlands and freezing temperatures in the West Country. There was an amusing incident on the morning Violet was to catch her train. Having taken uncle Reg an early morning cup of tea, she noticed his false teeth had frozen in the glass by his bed. Doris provided a delicious cooked breakfast but Violet wondered how she managed the household chores as the cottage had no modern appliances. Reg was likeable and excellent company but very mean.

On the train journey to Birmingham, Violet relived the precious time with Henry. She had felt safe in his deep love for her.

'Are you still seeing that naval lad?' Henry had asked. 'Is he serious about you?'

'He seems quite keen but I just enjoy dinners in a London restaurant and his company.' Violet wondered if Henry could tell that she had lost her virginity. The girls at the hostel discussed their boyfriends and who had done what physically. Three of the girls in the dormitory were no longer virgins.

Chapter 7

The first term was thrilling with concerts, performances and seminars with famous musicians. She registered with an Employment agency and the first job was in the perfumery department of Derry & Toms in Kensington High Street. The hours were long as well as all day Saturday and the only advantage was the purchase of reduced expensive perfume.

'Can you type or write shorthand?' asked the receptionist at the Agency.

'No, but if I learn will the pay be better?' replied Violet.

'Yes, and it would be only for five days, no Saturdays.'

Violet immediately enrolled in a secretarial evening class and within a few months the Agency sent her to work in various offices. The hours were shorter so she could practise the piano. The caretaker at the Royal College allowed Violet to play late evenings and weekends and he and his wife were sympathetic to Violet's problem of having to work in the holidays to pay for her hostel room.

Several of the companies she worked for offered Violet a full-time job as she was so efficient. There were luncheon vouchers at some of the offices and Violet was invited to social events from the staff.

The winter months in the hostel room were cold as there was only a small gas fire that consumed coins at an alarming rate. The girls often huddled by the fire eating chips before going to bed with hot water bottles but the hostel had an interesting aspect. Kensington was an expensive area in which to live so there were famous personalities in residence including Winston Churchill who lived close by. During Ascot week the girls saw well known entertainers leaving their homes in elegant clothes.

Violet became friendly with another girl in the hostel who worked in a branch of Lloyds bank. They were to become lifelong friends. Evelyn had come to London to find a husband and end a relationship with a married man. They talked about getting married and their previous relations with their married men. Violet described her love for Henry and they consoled themselves over a bottle of liqueur. Not knowing how much you should consume, they drank several glasses and were very sick during the night. 'I have a pain in my side,' complained Violet.

'The result of drinking all that alcohol,' replied Evelyn.

'It has been hurting for a while. Do you think I should see a doctor?'

'Wait for a few days and see if it goes,' suggested Evelyn.

Violet eventually arranged a visit to a doctor in Gloucester Road. He was Swiss and had many famous patients, including musicians and film stars. 'Check yourself into St George's hospital at Hyde Park Corner immediately; you need to have your appendix removed.'

Violet ran back to the hostel, collected a toilet bag and nightclothes and then waited for a bus to take her to Hyde Park Corner. She had asked the Warden of the hostel to ring her parents and to tell the girls where she was. The operation went smoothly leaving Violet with a scar on her right side.

Her mother came to collect her after ten days and a fortnight at home in Birmingham enabled Violet to recover from the operation more quickly than staying in the hostel.

On her return to London she met the naval officer, Peter, who had continued their relationship so when on leave booked himself into a hotel to see Violet. 'Have you ever had Indian food?' he asked. 'There is a well known restaurant in Picadilly. I'll take you there next time I am in London.'

Veeraswamy was the oldest Indian restaurant in UK, established in 1926 by the great-grandson of an English General and an Indian Mughal Princess.

It had an opulent interior and Violet loved all the flavours of the numerous dishes. Her culinary experience had been one main dish followed by a pudding, except when the family were in France, so it was a delicious treat to be taken there.

The next three years were a combination of music lessons, practising for hours, concerts at the Royal College, and performances by famous musicians. Violet loved the ballet and opera. She enrolled as a repetiteur at the opera school as she was required to have a second study. The violin had been disappointing in spite of Violet practising regularly. The cleaning lady put cotton wool in her ears if Violet was playing when she cleaned their room. The College librarian, often a formidable woman, had a soft spot for Violet and provided free tickets for Sadlers Wells and Covent Garden performances. For some of the performances Violet had to queue early in the morning and then after a couple of hours was given a ticket to queue for the actual seat. Seeing Margot Fonteyn dance with Rudolph Nureyev was a thrilling spectacle, watching his amazing leaps. The rapport between the two was obvious and in spite of Fonteyn being over 40 years old she was superbly supple.

Two opera performances remained a lifelong memory for Violet. Maria Callas was singing the title role in Zefferelli's production of Puccini's *Tosca*. Maria Callas wore the famous red velvet dress and at the end of the second Act when she stabs Scarpia there seemed to be a frozen silence in the audience.

There were noticeable tearful faces in the bar during the interval and Violet could still feel the emotion in her throat in spite of drinking tonic water.

The other memorable performance was seeing Joan Sutherland sing in Lucia di Lammermoor. She had a cold but insisted on giving a performance. Violet went backstage for her autograph and Joan Sutherland appeared still in her blood-stained robe from the opera. Her friendliness impressed Violet and the treasured signed programme were placed in a special folder. Being a Richard Wagner enthusiast Violet wanted to see one of the operas from The Ring cycle. She finally obtained a ticket but it was in the 'gods' and so she had a stool where she could follow the score but otherwise it was standing and sitting on the floor. Violet used her coat to sit on as the opera was nearly six hours long. When the girls heard about it they were amazed at Violet's stamina. 'That is true devotion to music,' said Sandra. Violet also bought a season ticket for the Proms in the Albert Hall every year. This also involved queueing as she wanted to be one of the Prominaders. Living close to the Albert Hall she starting queueing in the late afternoon, then others would take over while she went back to the hostel for a quick meal. When the doors opened there was a rush to reach either the front rail of the Promenade or a seat around the edge. She made many friends during the Proms season and Violet was impressed by their enthusiasm as most were working, not studying music. With all these concerts and opera performances her musical cup was brimming over.

'I think I have met my future husband,' said Evelyn one evening after dinner.

'What! Are you serious?' exclaimed Violet.

Evelyn had gone on a blind date with a friend at the bank where she worked. She had partnered the boyfriend's brother to a dinner and dance.

'He is in the RAF, I think, and wants to meet again next weekend.'

Within six months plans were going ahead for the wedding. Violet was asked to be bridesmaid and her skill with the sewing machine produced a beautiful lilac dress.

'I am now a married lady at last. Not madly in love but happy,' said Evelyn to Violet. 'You must think about your future and perhaps forget Henry. You seem to have a choice of three at the moment,' she said laughing.

The new admirer was a friend of Sandra's Pakistan boyfriend. He had worked in the Embassy but was now employed in Fleet Street at Reuters. Akbar was developing a serious attachment to Violet and they spent most weekends together. To her amazement, he accompanied her to Birmingham on a rare visit to her parents. They were surprisingly welcoming. Maybe as a preferable suitor to Henry, thought Violet.

Her letters to Henry were less frequent and she confessed to him to having a regular boyfriend. His reply expressed understanding, anxiety and love.

The bond between us is very strong and not at all likely to be broken. So my darling little one, again take care of yourself in every way.

They had managed to meet several times in Devon, Surrey and Bristol. When visiting Devon they always went to the coast as Violet missed the sound and smell of the sea in London. The Bristol rendezvous was a final realisation of their physical desires. Henry had booked a hotel for them to stay overnight. 'Are you anxious, my darling?' he asked. 'We have waited eight years for this moment.'

Their love making was intense but gentle. The passion expressed in intimate caresses and loving murmurs. After breakfast, the return to London was heartbreaking for them both and Henry was close to tears. The next letter expressed his feelings – '*My darling, to feel you so very much mine was an experience I have longed for years. I have loved you, my darling girl, for so long that were it not sincere and absolute then the "lustre would have dissolved" ere thus. Now my dearest and sweetest girl I leave you with the oft repeated words "I love you", so my love and my life, yours as always and forever, Henry.*'

Violet read it with tears running down her cheeks.

'He doesn't seem to make you happy,' remarked one of the girls. 'Perhaps you should end the affair – after all he is married.'

'I can't imagine living without him,' replied Violet, clutching a very damp handkerchief. She thought of the lines from the South Pacific song – 'Who can explain it, who can tell you why.

Fools give you reasons, wise men never try.'

Violet only felt the overpowering need to be with Henry although the age difference caused many disparaging comments.

She wrote a loving letter the next evening, enclosing a copy of 'Apart' by Patience Strong.

'Apart but still together, in the world of memory…you are never far away, and always in my heart. We know not when the hour of our reunion will be. But one day, someday, hand in hand we'll make another start.'

Violet felt the anguish of separation and likened her situation to the love between Robert Browning and Elizabeth Barrett. Her favourite poem was one of Elizabeth's sonnets – 'How do I love thee? Let me count the ways. I love thee to the depth and breadth and height, my soul can reach when feeling out of sight…I love thee with the breath, smiles, tears, of all my life…' She had visited the church in Marylebone where they were finally married. Would the future bring a happy ending for her and Henry?

Violet repeated the words of Shelley before she went to sleep that night – 'The fountains mingle with the river…Nothing in the world is single, All things by a law divine, in one another's being mingle – why not I with thine.' Another letter arrived within three days. Violet read the six pages when the dormitory was free of the other girls. She wanted to savour every loving sentence. Henry reminisced about their past meetings, but felt 'molto passionato con amore and very miserable' at their separation.

Violet had been bridesmaid at her sister's wedding as well as Evelyn's ceremony. A third wedding that year was the marriage of an uncle of Akbar at which Violet wore a blue and silver sari. She felt very elegant but sad. Her own happiness was still in doubt. She wondered whether her relationship with Akbar was one of compensation for the inability to be with Henry.

Chapter 8

Peter had now left the Navy and become a Civil servant. Violet thought that her remark about not wanting to be a naval widow while he was abroad had prompted his change of career. His reference to getting married at one weekend was received with a lack of enthusiasm by Violet as her heart and future plans were still with Henry.

The music studies were going well. Violet passed two diplomas and had a few hours each week giving piano tutorials at a teacher training college. The financial addition was essential to purchase piano scores. Henry had arranged a lesson for her with a famous composer and friend. She took the Schumann piano concerto and to her amazement the orchestral part was played by the composer on a second piano from memory. The experience became a lifelong memory.

Practising the piano during the summer holidays was difficult as Violet worked for the Agency during the day and attended the Prom concerts at the Albert Hall most evenings. Perhaps to earn more money teaching the piano might be the answer to the problem thought Violet.

Then a suggestion by one of the girls in the hostel solved the problem. 'How about moving into a flat?' asked Jennifer. She was also a Civil servant and very organised.

'There is one in Putney available for four tenants.'

Violet moved in with three girls that were not familiar to her but the opportunity to have her own room and perhaps even a piano was too tempting. To her surprise Akbar suggested looking for a piano. They found a second hand Bechstein upright and he helped with the finance. Putting the piano in her room was hazardous as there were three flights of stairs with a glass balustrade. They watched with bated breath but it went well and Violet celebrated with some brilliant piano solos. The journey to the Royal College was the only drawback but as there were only three sessions in her final year Violet was able to arrange a convenient timetable. Her life was extremely busy with lessons, teaching, part-time office jobs, concerts, auditions and her own performances. There was also the cleaning and cooking in the flat. Jennifer organised a rota for all of them and there was a party during the first month inviting the girls from the hostel dormitory and some of the boyfriends. It was noisy but great fun.

A letter to Henry suggested a visit to London so that he could stay overnight with her. He was delighted she had a piano on which to practise every day and at hours that suited her commitments.

I want to take you to the church in Surrey where I was organist although only a young boy. There might be a visit to my sister when I can spend some time with you.

The visit was arranged and Henry collected Violet from the flat. He drove to the small church and Henry held Violet in his arms by the organ.

A letter arrived two days later expressing his anxiety.

'Forgive, my darling, if I was "hungry" in the church. I hope kissing you there did not offend any principles. We were both pretty much of the same mind, I think, and that is all that needs to be said. It was good to re-affirm our love, darling. I don't see much sign of Diminuendo, do you? Here's to the next time, darling, and may it not be too long in coming.'

The final year was to prepare Violet for her Wigmore Hall debut. She had increased her repertoire considerably and hoped to perform a concerto with the Royal College orchestra. At the audition nerves caused her to make a small error of timing. A perfect performance was required so Violet did not give her concerto performance.

'Why do I feel nervous when I know the work so well from memory?' she complained to Akbar.

'You are only human and we all make mistakes. Your confidence will grow the more you perform,' answered Akbar.

There were several performances at Music clubs in London but often the pianos were in a poor state. One piano no longer had a sustaining pedal so Violet had to change her programme.

The girls in the flat gradually developed close friendships. Victoria was Welsh, Jennifer, the organiser, was Scottish and Olivia's home was in Carlisle. They all enjoyed listening to Frank Sinatra and Ella Fitzgerald as well as some jazz artists. Violet had been given money for a record player for her 21 birthday and, when finances allowed, she bought classical recordings. It was a struggle to pay the rent but she refused to ask her parents for any help as Violet needed to prove that she could manage to live in London independently.

Although she had a reserved, quiet personality, Violet attracted two new admirers. One was the best man at her sister's wedding and the other was the Head of Music at the training college. There was no physical development between them but Violet was treated to expensive seats at a Covent Garden opera performance in addition to some delicious restaurant dinners.

'Sinatra is performing at Hammersmith!' Jennifer shouted with excitement. 'We must get tickets.'

She managed to obtain four tickets and the evening before the performance was spent deciding what they should wear. When Sinatra finally walked on to the stage there was hysteria among the female audience. Violet and the girls cheered, shed tears and after the performance played his songs on the record player until the early hours. To be at a live performance would be remembered for the rest of their lives.

The weekends were usually spent with Akbar with occasional visits from Peter. He always stayed in a hotel as there was never an invitation to stay at the flat.

'Poor man,' said Jennifer. 'He could sleep on the sofa.'

'What about the morning when there are four girls using the bathroom,' replied Violet. 'He would be desperate for a pee waiting for us to finish.' They all laughingly agreed.

Henry wrote to Violet about the problems of marrying a man from a different culture and religious beliefs. His comments were related to Akbar as he realised the Asian was serious about Violet. She had no knowledge of his family in Pakistan only his friends in London. None of them were strict Muslims and there was no praying five times a day. Violet was not aware of any making the pilgrimage to Mecca – or the Hajj as the fifth Pillar of Islam was called. The only religious procedure was Ramadan, when Akbar and his friends fasted from sunrise to sunset. Violet would eat dinner at her usual time and Akbar, who was quite competent cook, would eat after sunset. His shift work at Reuters gave Violet a free weekend to see Peter. He caught a train from Yorkshire to London and spent a night in a Kensington hotel. They enjoyed a delicious meal and often attended a concert at the Festival Hall.

On one occasion the orchestra played the New World symphony by Dvorak which had special significance to Henry. Violet had shed tears during the first time she heard it and Henry had smiled but comforted her. She shed tears again but Peter assumed it was the music that had produced the emotion.

Both Peter and Akbar knew of Henry's attachment to Violet but not that her heart still ached for him. Because he was married and so much older than Violet, they considered Henry an unlikely future husband.

Chapter 9

During the final summer term at the Royal College disaster struck. 'I feel sick,' moaned Violet.

She thought maybe the curry had been too hot for her tender stomach.

A regular evening with Akbar in his rented room had been enjoyable, eating and watching television.

'Lie down and have a drink of water,' replied Akbar.

Violet was eventually sick and after a few hours fainted. Akbar had the sense to call an ambulance. It resulted in a painful ride to the nearby hospital where Violet was diagnosed with an ectopic condition. Instead of a normal pregnancy the foetus had lodged in one of the fallopian tubes.

'Stop the pain in my legs,' she cried.

'We are going to operate, dear,' said one of the nurses. Violet opened her eyes and felt a severe pain in her pelvis.

'You are a lucky lady,' said the surgeon, taking her temperature and blood pressure.

Apparently, her heart had stopped and her survival was due to their expertise.

'You will recover but we had to remove one of your ovaries so future pregnancies might be difficult.'

Violet had no idea that she had been pregnant and had never had plans to marry and have children. Her only thoughts about the future were to have a career as a concert pianist and make Henry proud of her.

The following weeks were a nightmare. Violet developed jaundice and there was another operation. Her regular nurse was a West Indian lady who treated Violet with motherly care. As she recovered she was allowed visitors.

Olivia had informed her parents who were relieved at her survival but furious with the man who had made her pregnant. They finally decided it was Peter but no one was going to do a DNA test. The other patients in the ward were surprised at the number of male visitors when her sister's best man and the music teacher brought flowers and then Akbar and Peter brought fruit.

Eventually, Violet was transferred to a convalescent home in Surrey where she could write to Henry. He was appalled at her suffering and the operations but was unable to visit her. His loving letter was a comfort and a reassurance of his constant love for her.

She had lost two stone in weight and his comment 'It will be difficult to see you on the horizon' amused Violet. He also mentioned 'places I pass on occasion that will always recall our "purple passion".'

He hoped she would manage a trip to Devon when she was fully recovered. There was the usual holiday in Bournemouth for him and his wife but '*although the food and rest are good you happen to be my life, darling, and whether at work or play you are ever in mind, and my darling girl "I love you".*'

Violet wrote a letter with a poem that she hoped Henry would appreciate.

The flame still flickers in the constant heart
Like a fire burning steadily in a tended hearth
The warmth it gives out reaches out to thee
Come closer, my love, and be warm with me.
That forbidden garden where once our hearts soared high
With flaming passion in eyes that shone with love
Now the mind treads gently down those paths
All passion buried deep within our souls.
Only still the eyes burn with love, which no time can dim their burning coals.
Like winter's slumber it lies within
To awaken to a forbidden heart – is it a sin?

Violet received another letter the same week in which Henry referred to the Elegy he had composed for a departed friend.

'*It could be so very much better for you, darling, "for remembrance". I could write for hours, Violet darling, and if I continue in reminiscent vein there is no telling when I shall stop.*'

To her delight and surprise Violet learned she had won the coveted Countess of Munster Award at the Royal College. It would give a year in Paris studying with a pupil of Maurice Ravel. The award did not cover accommodation in Paris so she needed to find a thousand pounds to pay for lodgings in the French capital. It was not to be. Violet finally settled for an extra year studying with the senior professor at the Royal College.

The girls in the flat were pleased Violet was not going abroad but were sympathetic at her missing the opportunity to study at the Paris Conservatoire. Her part-time teaching continued in addition to a few concert performances. The aim was still to give a debut recital at the Wigmore Hall. Christmas was spent in Birmingham with her family. Her sister had given birth to a daughter so being "Auntie Violet" would feel strange but exciting.

It reminded Violet of the year Evelyn was expecting her first child. Violet had made an attractive maternity dress for her to travel to Aden as her husband had been posted abroad. Evelyn was flying out to him on her own and she wanted to arrive looking elegant. As the plane took off Violet wondered how long it would be before she saw Evelyn again.

The news that arrived in the New Year was devastating – and would initiate a totally different direction for Violet's life.

Henry's wife had died on Christmas Eve. She was over ten years older than Henry and had suffered a heart attack.

I feel lost and very lonely, he wrote.

Violet did not know how to respond. The address in the letter was new to her and there was no telephone number. She wrote a sympathetic reply asking if the son, Daniel, was taking care of the funeral arrangements. Violet had never met him but he seemed a caring son based on remarks by Henry.

Violet appreciated the feeling of loss that Henry felt as it would be impossible to spend all those married years together and raise a son without having a deep attachment. Violet had met his wife on many occasions during her piano lessons with Henry and also at some of the Music competition festivals. When the relationship between Henry and Violet was discovered and she stopped having piano lessons from him, Henry told his wife the feelings he had for Violet. As a consequence their marriage was never such a contented one.

That Spring Violet was being examined at the Royal Academy of Music for a Performer's Diploma. The programme had to be technically and musically demanding as well as being from memory. The chosen Beethoven sonata had been selected in relation to Violet's private life. Les Adieux Op 81a always reminded Violet of her feelings when she left Devon and Henry for Birmingham. The agony of departure seemed to perfectly express in the slow movement. She was successful and immediately contacted Henry to arrange a visit to celebrate. Akbar and Peter were suddenly "on hold" and she caught the train to Exeter.

To spend three days and nights together after ten years of waiting seemed like a dream come true. The bungalow was small but the studio had a Steinway grand piano and a Bluthner upright piano. Henry listened to her playing with a critical yet appreciative ear.

'The full-time studies have certainly made an impact, darling. Don't look quite so anxious as if you are afraid of playing a wrong note. Enjoy the music so your musicianship and artistry come through.'

They enjoyed some two piano repertoires although the arthritis in Henry's hands imposed some limitations. Henry appreciated all the domestic help and cooked meals that Violet provided but he did have a regular cleaning lady who was named Widow Twankey by Violet. She was willing to help Henry by doing any extra chores needed and seemed pleased Henry had a love in his life.

A letter arrived two days after Violet returned to London.

It was all so 'as it should be' and so natural. Again I say, my darling, that this love of ours is intended, having lasted all these years and now coming to happy fruition.

Chapter 10

The girls wanted to hear all the details and what Violet intended to do about the romance.

'Are you going to marry him? What about Akbar and Peter?' asked Jennifer.

'I am spending Easter with Henry in Bournemouth. He has booked a week at this expensive hotel facing the sea and we will be hearing the Bournemouth Symphony orchestra in the Winter Gardens.'

The week in the hotel was one of joy as well as luxury. The staff were surprised at the age difference between Violet and Henry and also at his request for a double bed. One occurrence was totally unexpected. The hotel had a Casino so guests from other hotels arrived after dinner to play the tables.

'Oh no,' whispered Violet. 'I have just seen my sister's mother-in-law. She always stays at the Carlton hotel so she must be here for the Casino. She will report back to Birmingham and my parents.'

'I will tell them I still love you and plan to make your future a happy and successful one,' replied Henry.

Her parents were duly informed of Violet being with Henry in the hotel and were appalled but Violet was so overwhelmed at being with Henry after so many years that she ignored her parents' comments. The following week was spent in Devon confirming their deep love for each other.

Henry drove Violet to Exeter to catch her train back to London. He wrote the following morning, *My own darling Violet, First I feel I must say 'thank you' for all you gave me through the most wonderful two weeks of my life. The tears would come at the station as you left and I thought of all you mean to me. My pride and love grew each day, darling, until now it is just swallowing me up completely. I love you as it is rarely given to a man to love a girl and if you can accept this love, in spite of the many drawbacks, then it is yours, my darling. I shall always love you and cherish you, and indeed be true.*

The following months were spent preparing for concerts and auditions. The part-time teaching paid the rent and the girls were a great comfort. Henry wrote frequently giving encouragement to persevere with her concert career. He managed a few visits to the flat but it was tiring to drive to London and return to Devon the next day. On two occasions Violet felt unable to leave him at Sunbury where she usually caught a bus back to Putney. The need to be with him was so intense. The parting at Exeter the next day was tearful. 'Somehow my dearest, we are closer to each other than ever before and I am still hoping that we will eventually make it.'

Akbar and Peter had both proposed marriage to her in spite of Violet's love for Henry. The girls were also enjoying serious relationships. Olivia saw a dentist regularly but he was married, Victoria's boyfriend was an architect and Jennifer was experiencing an affair with a married policeman.

They sympathised with each other and listened to Sinatra and Ella Fitzgerald for consolation.

The summer vacation arrived and instead of working for Temps Violet decided to spend the weeks with Henry. The blissful weeks in the bungalow passed too quickly. They visited all their favourite places in the new MG Magnette. Henry loved his new car and hoped Violet would learn to drive. There was a financial need to pay the rent so Violet increased her teaching hours as well as taking office jobs for Temps on her return to London. Several letters arrived from Henry but one was especially loving. *Six weeks of heaven have left their mark, darling. I loved you deeply before, but now my love for you is just complete and overwhelming. It swamps my thoughts even when working and when not, it is almost too much. Tears will come, my love, even as I write for I feel that never was a man so blessed with love as was I during our summer.*

It was a joy to talk on the telephone and say goodnight to each other. Living with Henry raised a vital question for Violet. Could she continue her concert career in Devon? She had always believed that it was essential to live in London for the contacts and opportunities to perform. Henry's last letter was asking her to live with him permanently.

Violet darling, you are just my world and I want to marry you. In spite of the objections and disadvantages I'll wait, my precious one, and always love you to the end.

A decision had to be made by Violet as Henry for financial reasons could not move to London. His teaching practice was lucrative and his reputation was based in the West Country.

'What are you going to do?' asked Olivia. 'Your parents will be furious. You could find a piano teaching post in

London, continue performing at the Music Clubs and still see Henry regularly.'

Victoria thought marrying someone so much older was a mistake. 'What will his son say? He might stop seeing his father. Have you talked to Henry about all the possible problems?'

'When we are together nothing else seems important,' answered Violet. 'I want to live with him.'

The reply to her letter was everything Violet had hoped.

Your letter was pretty wonderful, darling, and I will do all I can to make you happy. So, my precious one, COME!

Arrangements were made for the move to Devon including the Bechstein piano. Violet spent a final weekend with both Akbar and Peter. They decided to join forces to persuade Violet to stay in London.

'They have gone to a pub to console each other,' said Jennifer. 'Not many women would have three men to choose from for a husband. What do you have that we don't?'

'I have no idea, perhaps you should have piano lessons!!!' Violet laughed. The girls arranged a farewell party. Jennifer did the cooking and there was plenty of wine. They planned to keep in touch and for visits to Devon the following summer.

Henry wrote his last letter to Violet in London arranging to collect her in the MG.

The very much longed for days are near at hand, my darling. I love you so deeply that my thoughts of being with you are totally joyous ones. I never cease to marvel at your love and kindness. On the upward journey I'll have you to look forward to and on the return you beside me.

Part 3
Sunhaven

Chapter 11

'Do you feel at home, my darling?' asked Henry.

'I always feel at home with you, my love,' replied Violet.

They had been living together for three weeks and a routine had been established whereby Violet practised in the mornings in the studio, with Henry suggesting recital programmes and discussing interpretation of the piano pieces. He commenced his teaching session at teatime and finished at nine o'clock in the evening. Supper followed with some television viewing and then to bed.

They often listened to classical music and for Violet to be surrounded by love and music every day was like a dream come true. The neighbours were friendly but surprised at Violet's arrival. The age difference always produced a reaction. Friends that Violet had known before she moved to Birmingham were pleased at her return to Devon, especially as she was giving piano recitals.

The sad situation with her parents was the only "minus" as they sent most of her belongings to the bungalow and stated that they would no longer be in touch. Her mother had included all the Press cuttings and programmes of Violet's concert performances but some of the concert dresses were missing. As she had her own sewing machine now Violet could make new concert outfits when needed. Henry was sympathetic with regard to the parents' attitude but for Violet the joy of being with Henry outweighed any drawbacks.

'Can we fix a date for our wedding day?' asked Henry. 'I would like it to be before Christmas.'

'How about on your birthday at the beginning of December,' suggested Violet.

'We need to give the Registry Office several weeks' notice, darling.'

The only members of the family present would be Henry's son and Violet's step-sister and her husband, Martin.

'You are looking very happy,' said Joan. 'Treasure the love you and Henry have and ignore the rest of the family.'

There had been a disastrous meeting with Henry's daughter-in-law. She came to tea with Daniel and their daughter, and Violet was treated to icy silence. Joy by name but not by nature, she refused to acknowledge Violet much to Dan's embarrassment.

'I am so sorry, Violet,' said Dan, apologetically. 'You know I am delighted you are marrying Father. He looks so happy.'

The wedding ceremony was a quiet affair with a celebration lunch at a hotel, and tea with cake at Sunhaven afterwards.

'What would you like as a wedding present, darling?' asked Henry. 'Apart from me!!!'

'Can we have a puppy?' Violet loved animals especially the dog belonging to one of her aunts. Reverie was a golden retriever and Violet made a wish while she was still at school to have one of her own when she grew up.

The six month old puppy was duly named Tristan after the hero in the Wagner opera and his attachment to Violet was immediate.

'He's crying,' said Violet. 'Can we bring him from the kitchen into the hall?'

'He will settle down soon and go to sleep,' replied Henry, during the first night that Tristan was at Sunhaven.

The next morning Tristan had chewed the wallpaper in the kitchen to reach them in the bedroom.

'I'll decorate and repair the plaster,' said Violet. 'He just needs to be with us at night.'

Fortunately, after that first night the dog settled down each night in the kitchen on his cosy rug. Violet gave him extra attention each morning and several food treats midday.

'Do I have a serious rival?' asked Henry. 'He follows you everywhere.'

'At least he is less demanding than a baby,' replied Violet laughing.

Life at Sunhaven continued with preparation for future recitals, trips to the moors to exercise Tristan, and their joyous union. The cleaning lady, called Widow Twankey by Violet, came every week and Henry had a regular gardener. The bungalow had been built on a plot of land that had been an orchard and there was a stream running through the front garden. Violet began her horticultural journey the following summer by watching the fruit and vegetables ripen. She learnt how to pickle onions, make jam from the strawberries and cook traditional meals from the vegetables. There was a butcher at the top of the road so meat was available without the need to drive to a shopping centre or market.

'Henry, are you impressed with my domestication?' asked Violet.

'You are my perfect cook, darling, but go easy on the clotted cream.'

Violet had a weakness for sweet food and clotted cream was served regularly on fruit or scones for tea.

'How would you like to boost the bank balance by giving some music lessons?' asked Henry.

'Just two or three pupils after 4 pm. when you start teaching would be fine but I must have my mornings free to practise and walk the dog.'

Violet had decided to add her grandmother's name to her performing name as it was fashionable to have a double-barrelled surname if you were a performing artist. As Violet Eden-Welby she gave a recital at the Lord Mayor's Christmas fund concert and was reminded of the Lord Mayor's concert when she was 13 years old. The following years Violet was invited to be guest artist at a variety of concerts. There was also a tour with a famous soprano that included a television appearance.

Mayflower 70 was a celebration of the pilgrims sailing from Plymouth to America. Violet appeared with international artists giving a solo recital and she felt so much pleasure at Henry's applause after the final encore.

As well known musicians their marriage was no longer regarded as an oddity, unlike the first year when a local reporter called at Sunhaven.

'Was the gate open when you arrived?' asked Henry. 'Well shut it on your way out.'

The press had wanted photos of them but there was just a small paragraph in one of the national newspapers. The repercussion of Henry's lack of cooperation was the omission of his name when his pupils achieved success in examinations and music festivals.

A new experience for Henry was a trip to Spain. Dan was a fluent Spanish linguist and visited Spain every year. He drove through France but Violet decided to go by ferry to Bilbao and then drive across Spain to the Mediterranean Sea. She took Spanish evening classes for six months and also passed her driving test. The ferry crossing was unpleasant as numerous passengers were sea sick and the accommodation was less than basic. The drive across Spain was exciting especially when they saw the young bulls at Pamplona. Violet could not face seeing a bullfight and wondered how anyone could bear to see the bull killed. Driving across Spain was an adventure for both of them but particularly for Violet. As a relatively new car driver, having passed her test the previous year, she had to remember to drive on the right side of the road. Barcelona was busy but they made a brief stop to do some shopping. The hotel on the Mediterranean coast was perfect with its own beach and a first class restaurant. They swam every day and relaxed on the beach under the straw umbrellas. The return journey to Bilbao for the ferry home went smoothly and Violet took a different route closer to the Pyrenees. There was an improvement in the food on board and the sea was calm across the Bay of Biscay.

'Did you enjoy that trip?' asked Violet. 'Or was it too arduous and strange?'

'It was certainly an experience but as long as you are with me I can travel anywhere,' replied Henry.

Tristan was very glad to see them and be back at Sunhaven. Violet gave him extra treats and longer walks.

When they stayed at a hotel he insisted joining her in the swimming pool so he had to be kept on a lead or left in the car when she went for a swim. In the sea Tristan seemed to think Violet needed saving but his paws pressing down on her shoulders resulted in a quick swim to safety. It was always a joy to watch him running along a beach and fetching a stick from the sea.

Violet kept in touch with the girls in the flat. Victoria had married her architect and was going to Venezuela; Jennifer had a wedding date to her policeman and Olivia decided to return to the North where she married a local young man from Carlisle.

Chapter 12

Whereas Henry knew everything about Violet's early life, she had no knowledge of his younger years. 'Tell me about your school days and what you did as a teenager,' said Violet one evening.

'There was no such thing as a teenager, you were either at school or you worked, or both,' replied Henry.

'My father owned a bakery and as a boy I helped with the bread delivery on the horse and cart. I made some of the deliveries before school in all weathers. There were occasions when the woman of the house paid "in kind" so I had to wait outside on the cart. If it rained I got soaking wet. Hence, the rheumatoid arthritis later in life.'

Violet was horrified at the ill treatment of Henry as a boy. His talents on the church organ and piano were not encouraged by his parents as his father was determined to keep Henry working in the bakery.

'I eventually decided to join the Marines and learnt to play the bassoon. I also gave piano lessons to some wealthy pupils in Surrey and played for the silent films. It was fun as I had to describe action, romance and humour in the choice of music so I often composed my own.'

'That is amazing. You were so young!' remarked Violet in astonishment. Henry then related how he played in the Marines but wanted to have his own orchestra. He eventually left the marines and moved to Devon where he formed a dance orchestra.

'We played regularly at the Royal Hotel,' he related to Violet. 'The Palm Court had a vast glass domed roof supported by marble columns and underneath were tubs of palms that were specially imported from Las Palmas.'

'Did the orchestra play for dancing or just for listening?' asked Violet.

'Both, we played for tea dances in the afternoon and Saturday evening dances, but often people just sat and listened with drinks,' replied Henry. 'It was the place to be seen especially those who wanted to be noticed. The entrance had a door draped with mandarin silk and the leatherwork was Japanese in green and gold.'

Henry was very tactful about his first marriage and just described the move back to Surrey as a result of the bombing in Plymouth during the war. Their house on the Hoe had been badly damaged to such an extent that it was eventually demolished and sadly the grand piano was also totally wrecked.

'But often something good comes from a disaster and I spent three years studying with Tobias Matthay,' said Henry with a smile. 'I met and became friends with many of his famous pupils. You know his The Act of Touch influenced piano pedagogy throughout the English-speaking world.'

Violet had met Myra Hess and Harriet Cohen, both pupils of Matthay, in Birmingham and the former artist had advised

Violet to follow a concert career 'only if it brings you happiness'.

Tobias Matthay, or "Uncle Tobs", had been a professor at the Royal Academy of Music in London, then he opened his own Pianoforte School in Oxford Street, and later moved to Wimpole Street. Violet thought how different Henry's life would have been if his father had encouraged his gifted son to study music when he was a young boy. Henry would have become an international concert pianist and a composer. He had composed a violin Sonata and an Elegy for clarinet and orchestra, both of which had been given public performances.

Violet wanted to share every activity with Henry so they watched the local football team in the winter, often with a blanket around their legs and a thermos of hot tea. In the summer, weekend afternoons were spent at the main cricket club where Violet took Tristan for a long walk in the adjoining park and then returned to a delicious cream tea. Henry was talented in golf and he had been a "scratch" player before retiring from matches. His other sporting skill was at the snooker table, and Henry had a photo of himself and Joe Davis playing a match in which Henry was the winner. The members of the snooker club would frequently play music while Henry was playing as that was the one thing that could distract him from a game.

'I have had a letter from my parents, darling, at long last,' said Violet. 'They are retiring and moving to a bungalow in Paignton.'

'Do they want to visit us or see you?' asked Henry.

'It would be good to see them after nearly three years of being ignored.'

'Perhaps they are finally accepting me as a son-in-law.' Henry laughed.

'Shall I agree to a meeting somewhere or an invitation to tea here, darling?'

'I think tea here would be best so they can see what a lovely home you have, my love,' replied Henry.

The reconciliation was cool but Henry was at his most charming and not embarrassed at showing his deep love for Violet.

'Evelyn has a son,' said Violet. 'They are living in Germany but will be back in the UK next year.'

The occasional letter and telephone call kept her in touch but it would be sometime before they met again. Violet no longer heard from the girls in the flat and she wondered what they were doing and if they had any children.

The years passed with another trip to Spain and several holidays in the UK. Henry always enjoyed an expensive hotel but Violet had to find ones that allowed dogs as Tristan only went into kennels when they went abroad.

Tristan had to be with Violet so when she went into the hotel swimming pool Tristan jumped in as well. She tried to dry him before he shook his wet fur over the other guests. One holiday in Budleigh Salterton was memorable as Tristan after a long walk across the golf course jumped into the hotel pool splashing all the guests who were quietly reading their Sunday papers. They were both busy with teaching as Violet had increased her number of pupils using her Bechstein in the living room. Henry's pupils continued to be successful in examinations and competitions in addition to three of them broadcasting for the BBC on the radio, confirming his reputation as the best piano teacher in the West Country.

Henry advised Violet on her choice of recital and concert piano pieces that she played to an international concert pianist in London just before her performances. This helped to give Violet more confidence as she still felt very nervous before a performance.

Her love for Henry was still the centre of her world and they enjoyed celebrating birthdays and anniversaries. A favourite restaurant was in Cornwall where, after a succulent steak, they had strawberries and cream. The clotted cream was brought to the table in a large bowl and Violet had difficulty in limiting her portion.

'How about a trip to Bigbury and Burgh Island?' suggested Henry.

'Yes, that would be lovely.'

It was autumn so most of the tourists had departed.

'We can cross to the island by the water duck if the tide is in,' said Violet.

She loved going there as Henry had driven there when Violet visited from London so it had a special meaning for both of them. It was a week after this trip that Henry fell sick. He had a cut on his arm that was slow to heal but he had not paid much attention to it. Violet cancelled the lessons for the rest of that day and called their doctor. He was one of Henry's adult pupils and prescribed Henry's medication. Violet had to leave a message as the doctor was out on an emergency call.

Violet contacted one of their neighbours, Greta, as Henry was losing consciousness. She was a practical woman whom Violet felt would do the best for Henry.

'We had better call an ambulance,' said Greta. 'I will look after Tristan while you are at the hospital.'

In the ambulance Henry gripped Violet's hand. 'I love you,' he whispered. By the time they reached the hospital he was looking very poorly and as they settled Henry into a bed, he went into a coma. Violet sat with him for two days with one brief trip home for a shower and fresh clothes.

'I am here, my darling.' Violet gave a heartrending cry as the love of her life stopped breathing.

The following days were a nightmare. Her parents arrived to support Violet and she was given medication to help her sleep. A pupil arrived from Cornwall for a lesson from Henry as she had not heard about his death. It was an upsetting incident and she had to be comforted and given a drink before returning to Cornwall. At the funeral the church was filled with shocked pupils and friends.

'Try to stop crying, dear,' said her mother, but Violet could not control the sobbing. How could she live without Henry, her heart was breaking.

Apart from the trauma of losing Henry, there was the problem of his pupils. Violet decided to teach them herself if they wished as she needed the income.

The ensuing nine months passed with teaching, several concerts which Violet dedicated to Henry and so played brilliantly but with an aching heart, and walking Tristan. Violet buried her grief in hours of teaching and piano practice, but needed the medication to enable her to sleep. Dan was always at hand and her parents telephoned her most weeks.

Violet had not written any poems during her marriage to Henry but one afternoon in the garden she had a desire to compose some lines.

What shall I remember when the trees are stripped and stark

Standing close beside you in the garden hushed,
This I will remember to lighten winter's dark.
This beauteous Nature that surrounds us
These blinding scenes we behold
Will love be so abundant?
Will thy love be so abundant?
Will thy heart sing still when old.
Those puffy clouds against skyline move
Their changing patterns sliding still what do they hide?
From blazing dawn to bloody sunset are ye so small beside?

She recalled Henry's love of the country and sea, and his appreciation of Nature and the changing seasons. They both had a love of beauty in all life around them, not just in music.

Chapter 13

The summer examination session was the first Violet had experienced. There were five grade eight pupils as well as lower grades. As the session took several hours the associated board examiner was booked for the whole day at Sunhaven.

He was friendly and impressed by the number of advanced candidates. Violet provided lunch and during the afternoon session while the candidates were watching Wimbledon tennis matches he joined them for a short time. He knew of Henry's reputation and expressed his condolences to Violet, saying what a loss his death was to the music profession.

After the total success of the examination candidates the summer vacation arrived with Violet at a loss without Henry. She decided to visit a number of National Trust properties. The buildings in Devon and Cornwall had been visited during previous years so she thought a trip to the north of England would be more interesting. Chatsworth and Castle Howard were on her list but she also planned to visit Blenheim Palace en route.

Tristan had been a constant companion and consolation although he hated Violet spending time at the piano. To recall her precious time with Henry was now too painful so she shut her mind to the memories.

On reaching Yorkshire Violet wondered if Peter still lived in Huddersfield. Perhaps I will write when I return to Sunhaven, she thought. The response was a complete surprise. Violet had expected him to be married with a family but his letter reminded her of their time together in London, their enjoyment of concerts as well as their intimacy. Violet considered that the invitation to visit him in Yorkshire would cheer her up but she did not want a serious relationship to start again. Peter had been very keen to marry her before she left London.

A trip to Yorkshire would be enjoyable as I love the Bronte books and Peter's parents lived in Haworth, thought Violet. There was a friendly welcome from his parents and they walked their dog with Tristan on the moors. They visited the Bronte home and Violet bought some pictures of the Bronte children as well as meeting the curator of the museum.

Peter reminisced about the London days. 'You know I went to the pub with Akbar when you left for Devon. We were both devastated by your departure,' related Peter.

'I can't talk about Henry,' replied Violet.

After the few days in Yorkshire, Peter wrote regularly. His love had been on hold but now it flourished with no restraint. *On Sunday I went up on the moors to that waterfall again and wanted you with me. I could almost feel your hand in mine. Remember I am here and thinking about you.*

By the end of the summer vacation the letters had become passionate. *Darling, I long to worship you with every gesture and every part of me – with every kiss and caress.*

They planned to spend a week in the family caravan but the weather was appalling with rain every day. Violet did not enjoy having a wet retriever sleeping beside her but Tristan loved the walks on the moors and had no problem with the wet conditions. After four days they decided to return to Haworth and dry out.

Peter had mentioned his plan to transfer to Devon in the Civil Service and although Violet wrote an encouraging letter she was nervous of embarking on a serious relationship so soon after Henry. To have another man feel so intensely about her again was frightening and she craved a quiet life with just her concerts and teaching to manage.

My dear heart, I need you and can only think of a complete life with you as my partner. I will love you all my life – as I feel I have for so long.

As she read this, Violet began to feel guilty about reviving her relationship with Peter. She did not feel any deep love for him only as a close and reliable friend and a gentle lover when needed. The letters continued to arrive with intimate expressions of his feelings for her.

Are you spending Christmas with your parents or will you come to Haworth and celebrate with me? asked Peter.

'Yorkshire it is,' replied Violet. She still enjoyed his company and his parents were very welcoming.

There was snow on the moors so walks were difficult. Peter's parents gave Violet a warm welcome again and the Christmas dinner was delicious. "Stay until January", pleaded Peter.

Violet needed to prepare for the winter term of teaching as well as resuming her piano practice. She suddenly realised that he was going to propose marriage on New Year's Eve.

The need to return to Sunhaven became urgent as her heart did not respond to Peter as it should if they were to become husband and wife. She knew no one could replace Henry.

'I have to go home. But will write and explain,' said Violet almost in tears.

'What have I done – or said!' exclaimed Peter. 'Tell me so I can put it right.' During the drive back to Devon Violet realised she had led Peter into believing she was serious about him. He had filled the loneliness without Henry but when she read his letters she realised she should have told him that there was no possibility of a marriage.

Violet arrived at Sunhaven feeling a sense of relief at being home. A letter arrived the next day from Peter before she had time to write to him.

It seems I have lost you again, my dearest darling. I loved the very presence of you with me and the times we spent together have been golden moments in my life. I wanted to continue past those golden gates into a wonderful life together. You have the makings of being a great teacher and performer, my love, but maybe you need more time before you settle down to married life again. I miss you very, very much and love you deeply and intensely.

Violet wrote a long letter explaining her feelings. To wait for her would be wasting his life, as sadly she did not feel the deep love for him. There was one final letter from Peter during the dark winter months in which he said his "goodbye".

Violet had several performances during the following months including a television appearance. Many of the Music clubs had inadequate pianos for a serious recital so Violet organised her own Steinway to be delivered. The local television station wanted to interview her about her "travelling piano".

There was a preparation session before the live broadcast and Violet talked about her concert career. She also mentioned how Tristan hated her playing the piano as it was a rival to her attention to him. In particular he disliked the key of C major and howled when Violet played any piece of music in that key. After the broadcast there were numerous phone calls about Tristan. His reaction to Violet's piano playing had caused quite a public interest.

Violet spent her leisure time in the garden. Watching the spring bulbs produce their array of colour always gave her pleasure and hope for the future. The summer vacation was spent painting the outside walls of the bungalow white. Violet was a not a fan of the previous pink walls.

'Making a good job there,' said a neighbour. 'Let me know if you need a tall ladder.'

The bungalow was built on a slope so there was a cellar under one half where all the garden tools were kept. It also provided storage for onions and potatoes. There was a problem with mice so Violet had to put down traps but had to take the damaged mouse to be killed to a neighbour as she could not kill it herself.

Just before the autumn term started she had a holiday invitation. 'Would you like to join us in Malta for two weeks?' asked Greta.

Her husband Luigi was Maltese and he was very kind if Violet needed any jobs done that she was unable to manage. They had a very young daughter who frequently visited Violet to be treated to breakfast or tea. She also loved seeing Tristan and stroking his head.

'I'd love to come but must arrange for Tristan to go into kennels.'

It was a glorious fortnight of sunshine, sightseeing and swimming. One of the brothers of Luigi was a priest and he arranged with the local radio station for Violet to broadcast some piano pieces. It was a short recital but the family were delighted at having a talented guest. The mother was a widow and there were two daughters and several sons, some who were working abroad. There were regular celebrations with fireworks and religious parades and on one occasion a firework factory exploded with a spectacular display.

Fortunately no one was injured. The fireworks reminded Violet of a firework display when she was very young. The neighbours in the cul-de-sac joined together for the November 5th celebration. The rockets were set in milk bottles before they were lit but one went through their front room window and set the curtains alight.

'Our Roddy dolls!' cried Violet. 'We must save them.' She had rushed into the house with her sister to rescue their dolls. The memory made her smile. Violet came back from Malta with a suntan and felt ready to start another academic year.

Chapter 14

Violet had several adult pupils who played advanced repertoire. There was a bank manager, a restaurant owner and a physics master at a boys' school.

The latter had studied with Henry. He was married with a teenage son and lived in Cornwall. He came into the city daily during term time so Violet arranged his lessons when he came into Plymouth to teach. He attended all her performances and also helped her choose a hi-fi system. As well as the Frank Sinatra records she had in London Violet had added an excellent collection of classical vinyl records that included orchestral as well as piano performances. Leonard was knowledgeable with regard to speakers, turntables and playing needles, and he installed the system for her.

He was an excellent Bridge player and suggested to Violet that she learn to play so she persuaded two friends to join her at evening classes. Bridge demanded concentration and a good memory and as Violet had both for her piano performances she thought she might be good at playing Bridge. The classes were sociable evenings so they provided another distraction from losing Henry.

By the Christmas holidays Leonard had become a good friend for Violet and during the following months they started a sexual affair. The sharing of music and Bridge became an important aspect to their relationship. As a married man their meetings were not regular and Violet was teaching most evenings during the week.

'I can come for lunch most weekdays,' said Leonard. So, lunchtimes became soup and sex and again it provided a distraction from Henry's absence.

'Your father is having a hip operation next month,' said her mother.

'Arrange a convalescent stay after the operation,' advised Violet. She knew how demanding her father could be. Violet visited regularly but she failed to persuade her father to abandon his zimmer frame.

'You must do daily exercises and move on to two sticks.'

But he became a permanent patient with her mother obeying every whim. To give her a break Violet insisted on two weeks in a convalescent home for her father. He was pampered and spoilt by the carers so enjoyed the brief stay. Her mother had a complete rest enjoying walks and free days without the constant demands from her husband. On one visit Violet heard a whistle. 'What is that?' asked Violet.

'He calls me by blowing the guards whistle he still has from the railways,' replied her mother.

'You are joking!!!' said Violet in amazement. 'I'll put a stop to that!' Violet then asked her father for the whistle.

'You are causing her so much stress rushing to see what you want every time you blow that whistle. Try to use sticks instead of the zimmer frame and do your exercises.'

Violet threw the whistle in the dustbin but her father just sat in his armchair without doing the exercises.

Early one morning the telephone rang while Violet was having breakfast. 'Your father died early this morning,' said her mother.

'I'll be there in the next hour,' replied Violet.

During the funeral, Violet could only think what a relief it would be for her mother. Although he had been a good provider for the family working overtime and not spending time in the pubs with colleagues, the last four years he had demanded constant care.

'You can sell the bungalow and move into a flat down by the sea,' suggested Violet.

'I have found the ideal one facing the sea front and close to all the shops,' replied her mother, a few weeks later. 'I can swim and walk to the music shop.'

Her mother had a part-time job doing the accounts in a local music shop. She was brilliant at mental arithmetic and never needed a calculator. She also loved to play scrabble so joined a group that played weekly in their homes. Violet saw the change in her mother and was delighted at the obvious contentment. When the tourists departed in the autumn, she went swimming with her mother and went on walks along the cliffs.

Violet had been looking for a larger house so she could have a separate studio for her pupils but eventually decided to build an extension to Sunhaven.

'There will be a separate entrance for the pupils so the rest of the bungalow will be more private,' she told Leonard.

'Will you keep all the pianos?' asked Leonard.

'No, I only need two and have found a buyer for the Bluthner upright.' Violet had designed the extension so that the two pianos, music library and furniture all fitted comfortably. She had used the builders who had built apartments near the waterfront on the river Plym. Leonard and his wife had decided to have separate homes, selling the house in Cornwall and Leonard had moved into one of these apartments. The arrangement with his wife was amicable and they still visited each other. Violet had met his wife on several occasions but as there was no question of a divorce their meetings were friendly. She was also a teacher and had a relationship with one of her colleagues. She told Violet that Leonard could be violent and at times made her feel nervous. The only occasion Violet had seen any aggression in Leonard was when a neighbour became a nuisance with his dog and called her offensive names. Leonard had physically pushed him against the garden wall, threatening him if he continued to bother Violet.

When the autumn term started, her pupils were amazed at the new entrance to the Studio. There was a new porch and all the windows and doors had been replace with double glazed UPC.

The pupils were achieving regular success at Music festivals and examinations so Violet was becoming well known as a piano teacher. It gave her joy to think she was following in Henry's footsteps. The only problem was the lack of time to practise for concerts so her performances were far less. She found the anniversary of Henry's death less painful each year but after listening to one of their favourite symphonies Violet put pen to paper.

What shall I do when you leave me?
How shall I feel when you go?
Will I weep and mourn
Will I kneel and pray

No – just take my heart, bleeding and torn.

There was still a problem with Tristan howling or whining when she played the piano. The vet diagnosed jealousy but also that without Henry the dog was guarding Violet. His devotion and protection was endearing but a musical dilemma. It was impossible to have him in the Studio so he spent the evenings banished to the kitchen.

Violet's literary talent was demonstrated in the programme notes for concerts and recitals. They were detailed and accurate as she had researched the items being performed. The local Press asked her to report all the local classical concerts and recitals so Violet interviewed the artists as well as meeting the Press deadline. Two of the international pianists came to Sunhaven to practise on the Steinway piano.

One of her close friends, Gordon, had been totally supportive after Henry died and both he and his wife were always on call. Gordon organised most of the classical performances in the city and was involved with the Leeds International Pianoforte Competition. All the finalists gave recitals and Violet chose their submitted programmes, wrote the programme notes in addition to entertaining them during their visit.

Her involvement with the Competition included visiting Leeds to hear the international competitors play in the early rounds. The two final rounds were televised live by the BBC and after the winner was announced Violet enjoyed the celebration supper. Although it took place every three years, she met the founder Fanny Waterman on several occasions and looked forward to going to all the events.

'It is a long drive to Yorkshire but we go shopping, do a little sightseeing, and the performances are so impressive,' she related to Leonard.

Violet had two Bridge friends and two from her school days and she discovered two of them were having affairs with married men.

When she was living in the flat in London Victoria was the only girl not having an affair with a married man. Two ended in a happy marriage but Violet now heard about two present affairs.

Her Bridge friend, Janet, had a teenage boyfriend whose mother was a close friend of her mother. As adults they both married someone else but kept in touch through their mothers. Janet finally had a sad divorce but Arnold had a family and was reasonably content. With her divorce Janet relied on Arnold for help in the house and garden when he visited Janet's mother.

Eventually their teenage relationship returned and a loving affair became part of their lives. It was in full flood when Violet became friends with Janet going to Bridge classes. Janet also had a musically gifted son to whom Violet eventually gave piano lessons.

The other friend from school days told Violet an amazing account of her affair. They played tennis on occasions and Violet taught Maggie's daughter the piano for a short time.

'We had been seeing each other occasionally and then he wanted to experiment with our physical relationship,' related Maggie.

'I had met his wife but she seemed very naive and obedient to her husband's demands.'

'What happened?' asked Violet.

'He wanted to have sex with both of us at the same time! I decided it would be fun but that he was joking. When I visited their house expecting him to be alone the wife was waiting in the bedroom.'

'What did you do?' said Violet in anticipation of a confrontation with the wife.

'She was willing but nervous,' replied Maggie. 'I undressed but suddenly decided I did not relish three of us being in bed having sex. So I put on my clothes and left.'

'Have you seen him since?'

'No, I have ended the affair.'

'Wise decision,' said Violet. She was appalled at the idea of sharing a sexual experience with another woman at the same time as the male lover.

Her relationship with Leonard continued but when he separated from his wife Violet suggested a break.

'Perhaps you should restore your marriage and stop seeing me for a while,' she suggested, although he was the major person in her social life and met her physical needs.

'How can I give you up when we experience so much pleasure with each other,' replied Leonard in a sad voice. 'I could just come for piano lessons but not touching you would be a problem.'

They agreed on a six month break, so as a distraction Violet decided to learn to sail. The lessons were a delight and she made progress within weeks.

Another member of the class was a medical scientist with whom Violet became good friends. Richard was intelligent and good company but Violet resisted his physical advances as she had had enough of a problem with Leonard.

'You have really taken to sailing – like a duck!!!' said Richard smiling. 'Are you going to buy a dinghy? The singlehanded Lasers are not difficult to sail.' Violet joined a sailing club and the following spring bought a Laser.

'I need to see you again,' said Leonard on the telephone. They had been apart for nearly six months when Violet learned he was having a sexual relationship with one of his regular Bridge partners.

'I think not,' replied Violet. 'You seemed to have found a replacement for me.'

'It was very brief and a complete disappointment. I only want you as my mistress.'

Leonard always called her M, for mistress and she called him L. He had given her large teddy bears and bought expensive gifts for her birthday during the preceding years. After much pleading he persuaded Violet to meet. The return to Sunhaven resulted in a torrid reunion.

Leonard decided to learn to sail and joined the same sailing club.

'We can sail together. I have seen a Fireball for sale at the club. You could helm and I can crew,' said Leonard.

He bought her a pink wet suit and she started winning some of the Laser races.

'You know why you are doing so well lately,' said Leonard. 'The men are staying behind to admire you in the pink wet suit.'

The next year was a fairly peaceful one for Violet with Bridge, sailing, piano sessions and concerts with Leonard. He enjoyed listening to her play some of her more difficult repertoire which made up somewhat for the musical gap left by Henry's absence.

Leonard was still visiting his wife regularly at her cottage and often stayed overnight but Violet was not anxious to remarry so this did not pose a problem for her.

'I have bought an eighteen foot yacht and it is moored near the apartment,' said Leonard, the following year. 'How about a few days at sea. Pack some warm clothes and bring some tinned food as the fridge is small.'

Violet loved living on the boat. There was a cooker, a shower and toilet, and the bunks were surprisingly spacious. Tristan seemed to cope with being on board, and as long as he was with Violet he was a happy dog. His only hate were the swans that came for food, especially when they reached into the boat. Tristan barked furiously as their long necks appeared over the side.

The trip along the coast was demanding but exciting and to Violet's delight and amazement they saw a shark. It was dozing in the sunshine and their boat sailed so close they could see its closed eyes.

The horse riding that Violet enjoyed in London continued on the moors. Some weekends she drove to a sheep farm on Dartmoor that also had stables. The wife of the owner had a superb Arab stallion and the other horses were all in excellent shape. Leonard could ride so they enjoyed galloping across the moors, then stopping at a pub, called The Elephant's Nest, for lunch, then riding back to the farm before tea. It was exhilarating and also kept Violet physically fit. Violet tried to take Tristan on one occasion but he found it difficult to stay with the horses and also showed his jealousy at Violet giving attention to another animal by barking furiously at them.

In the spring, some of the lambs needed to be bottle fed and Violet could not believe she was holding a lamb while it drank milk from a bottle.

'I cannot imagine how the farmer can kill them for the butcher,' complained Violet.

'It is their livelihood and killing reared animals is part of being a farmer,' said Leonard.

Chapter 15

Tristan was now over 13 years old and suffered with arthritis. He also worried Violet by disappearing for hours without her knowing where he was. She assumed he had found a home where they treated him with food and attention when Violet was teaching the piano. Often she had to drive around the neighbourhood looking for him or calling the police to ask if he had been injured. There was a long discussion with the vet as to a remedy.

'He is too old to go on a farm and the arthritis will not improve. Have you considered putting him out of his misery?' said the vet.

His running away became a real problem and Violet could only spend a limited time with him as she still continued to practise for concerts.

The decision had taken six months and she held Tristan as the vet injected the fatal dose. No canine welcome when she returned home was heartbreaking. She shed tears at losing her close companion but Leonard comforted her.

'He was suffering with arthritis in his joints and you had to lift him into the car when you took him for long walks. I know you will miss him very much but it was the right decision.'

The pupils were all very sad at the demise of Tristan and several brought presents to console Violet. There was a beautiful indoor plant and a shrub to plant in the garden in his memory.

To fill her leisure hours when she walked Tristan Violet decided to build another extension to Sunhaven. It would have a new kitchen, dining area, large bedroom ensuite and a utility area. She chose the colour schemes very carefully and the kitchen impressed a visiting international pianist when he came to rehearse on her piano. It had red worktops and the tiles were decorated with Japanese ladies in red, white and black kimonos. The tiles in the ensuite were lilac and pale green with a matching pale green floor covering.

Outside the area had new paving and steps with a wrought iron handrail to reach the lower level. The garden had acquired an extra piece of land as the farm fields below Sunhaven had been developed with numerous new houses and garages. When the access was closed off it gave a patch of ground covered in brambles and grass adjoining the garden, so Violet erected a fence and after a certain period of time it became part of her property.

She had met Freddie at the sailing club and he had taught her to sail a small yacht. He also ran a plant nursery so offered to assist Violet with her landscaping of the new piece of land. Violet drew the design of the area with a path, a paved area around the small pond and seating. She had found a large piece of slate in the cellar so Freddie had it cut for a seat and tops to the pillars at the bottom of steps to the paving. The stream in the garden disappeared through a large pipe so Violet had blocked it with a football and created the pool. She then bought a few fish to make the area more interesting.

When finished it added a sunny place to seat in the evening and relax outdoors.

'I am so pleased, Freddie,' said Violet. 'You have been a real treasure doing all the heavy digging and planting.'

'Well you know how special you are, my dear,' replied Freddie.

His soft spot for Violet resulted in a regular delivery of trout when he went fishing in his yacht – and poems.

Ode to the Garden of my Luv appeared the week after they finished the planting.

The church bells toll the knell of parting day
As filthy Fred wends home his weary way
Fred's filth is merely mud and mire
From labour with but one desire.
A Garden gem to build it seems
Which doth outdo the arty dreams
Of that comely wench who sits so sexily on my carved bench
As Fred with weary toil and brow a'wrinkled
Suddenly hears the ivories tinkled.
Tis Violet a haunting tune she plays on clavier,
Whilst Fred he snatches a well-earned rest to sit enraptured
As through his lug 'ole the tune he captured.
The poem continued for another verse and ended –
Now time it is to go to bed
As Fred doth lay his weary head
But sleep he yet but ne'er a nod
Thinks of Violet with comely bod.
Wot thinks he next he cannot tell
'Cos Vicar says he'll go to hell!!!

The poem made Violet laugh every time she read it and his affection for her was a great comfort. If she had any problems Freddie would always listen and try to help. He was a good teacher when they sailed but Violet teased him about the state of the boat and its lack of cleanliness. Another lengthy poem arrived the following week with a trout for dinner.

'Tis Friday and my heart goes out to Violet, she hasn't got a trout.

A fishless Friday she must pass

'Cos Fred the very selfish ass

Has gone a sailing o'er the water

To catch a whopper for Vi he'd "aughta" (poetic licence!) now Fred he dreams that were he but a trout

If Violet should cast her bait before his snout

He'd rise and take it, she need not fret

And 'fore he knew it, she'd have him in the net...

Fred, he's just a sporting type, there's nowt about him fishy

He just thinks our Violet is sweet and very, very dishy!

The garden produced fruit and vegetables but the pollen caused nasal problems for Violet.

'You have a small canal and we could remove a portion of the bone so that you could breathe more easily,' said the consultant.

'Can I have a new nose?' asked Violet. Both her parents had large noses and with recent television appearances, Violet thought a small nose would be more attractive.

'I will speak to the plastic surgeon and make an appointment.'

The nasal canal was enlarged and Violet had a neat, new nose. The only minus to the process were the two black eyes after the operation.

'You will have to wear sunglasses for a while,' said her mother with a smile. During the next few years the teaching career became full-time with only an occasional guest artist performance. Violet allotted one evening a week to Bridge, sailing the laser and Fireball in the summer and horse riding on the odd weekend.

Leonard's level of Bridge was far too advanced for Violet although he taught her various conventions that were interesting for her to try. Her card memory did not match her music notation memory. Violet had a photographic memory for her piano repertoire but when the Bridge sessions continued until late evening she lost her concentration and ability to calculate where the critical cards might be.

There were regular visits to her mother and step-sister. Joan had been diagnosed with Krone's disease so there was always anxiety over her condition. Martin was a very loving husband but the concern over his wife's condition caused a serious consumption of alcohol.

'Can you call in over the weekend?' enquired Joan on the telephone.

'Are you going into hospital again?' asked Violet anxiously.

'No, Martin has been diagnosed with cancer and has been given about six months.'

The funeral took place during the spring months. Violet had felt relief at her father's funeral but losing Martin brought uncontrollable tears. Joan possessed an inner strength that had enabled her to cope with her illness and this supported her during the ensuing months. Martin had discovered classical music late in life and talked about his discovery with Violet when they met for a drink. He had left her his complete set of Wagner's Ring Cycle and as she listened to the opening of Siegfried the loss prompted Violet to write a poem.

A carpet of crocuses protected from the crowd.
What a sight to feast one's eyes on
What ease to a furrowed brow.
As sunshine enhanced their purple hue.
My soul lingered with the scene
Was this only Nature's magic
Or is there a God supreme?
Clusters of golden daffodils bowing to the wind
My eyes beheld the glory, this blaze of springtime gold.
It soothed my fevered, straining mind
It seered my very soul.
There was a sudden easing of the aching heart
A feeling of momentary calm
But its swiftness in passing left a sadness
All too sharp – not a balm.

Chapter 16

Violet had two other admirers in addition to Freddie – her accountant, Jack and an adult pupil Ryan. As a self-employed musician Violet organised her accounts at the end of each academic year and Jack sent them to the Tax office with the correct forms. He was very efficient and over the years they became good friends. His secretary always welcomed Violet with coffee and asked about her concerts. On one occasion there was a refund from the Tax office so Jack suggested celebrating with lunch at a nearby Chinese restaurant. Back at the office the secretary gave Violet a bright smile as well as a questioning look. Unknown to Violet, Jack had been viewing her in a romantic way and the secretary was expecting her boss to propose over lunch. There was no proposal but at their next meeting Jack explained.

'I was planning to arrange a few outings for the two of us but I know you object to my cigarette smoking. I was considering giving up the cigarettes if my overtures to you were successful.'

'Goodness, I had no idea you were romantically interested,' replied Violet. 'You are a dear friend, Jack, but any more intimate involvement is out of the question.'

'I will continue as your accountant of course, and if you need an escort for any of the concerts or evening dinners, let me know. Purely as a caring friend,' said Jack with certain regret in his voice.

The other admirer, Ryan, was one of Violet's advanced pupils owning a restaurant in the town. He was a superb patisserie chef and Violet was often treated to delicious gateaux. When she was shopping in the city there was always coffee and cakes with Ryan's favourite piano music, Chopin, playing in the background. He was married with three sons so had a busy life but 'my most enjoyable time is my weekly piano lesson with you,' he told Violet.

Another pupil reminded Violet of Henry. He was a young marine who needed lessons on the musical paperwork for his enrolment in the marine band. She recalled Henry's account of his days in the Marine band at Chatham. The young Marine recorded the lessons on a tape recorder so that he would not forget any information Violet imparted.

The relationship with Leonard continued with Violet enjoying all their activities together. Another trip in the boat was suggested so a route was plotted on the charts, food and water loaded and some extra warm clothes. Although it was the summer, evenings and early mornings could be chilly.

One early morning Violet came on deck and saw a kingfisher perched on the stern rail. Because the boat had a bilge keel it could moor in river estuaries and sit on the mud when the tide went out, so seeing wildlife became an added pleasure. But the enjoyment ended when they returned to the moorings near Leonard's flat.

'Shall we have dinner at a restaurant or back at your flat?' asked Violet. 'Well, the flat is awkward as my wife is staying there.'

'What is going on between you two?' shouted Violet. 'I thought you just visited her after Bridge or to see your son.'

She gathered up her belongings and stormed off the boat in the dinghy. The news that Leonard and his wife had moved in together after all these years was too much for Violet. There had also been another affair that Leonard had lied about the previous year. A teaching colleague also sailed and Leonard had taken her out in the Fireball resulting in a sexual relationship.

'You are constantly deceiving me. I can never trust you,' cried Violet over the telephone. She refused to see him in person afraid she would attack him in her anger and misery. Violet wanted a stable relationship not necessarily leading to marriage, but certainly not including other women. 'I think I need to change my life,' she said to Joan.

'Well, Leonard is definitely not good enough for you. His cheating and deception seems to be part of his personality,' replied Joan. 'He certainly lacks Henry's qualities.'

'I have made enquiries about teaching the piano abroad. Malaysia apparently has a large number of music schools and the Associated Board sends examiners for several weeks annually for all instruments. I am going to book a holiday to explore the possibility of teaching there.'

There was yet another reunion with Leonard and he was excited about joining Violet on her Malaysian holiday.

The luxury hotel in Kuala Lumpur (KL) exceeded her expectations. The outdoor pool was a joy and as they sat having a delicious evening meal, Violet thought her decision to come to Malaysia with Leonard was proving to be a good one. They hired a sightseeing guide and David took them to all the sights – a tea plantation, Malacca and Penang. There was also time by the sea at Kuantan. Violet loved the temples, the warm sea and the food. The only disappointment was the lack of teaching posts at the music schools.

David suggested a few days in Thailand before their departure from Kuala Lumpur.

Bangkok was fascinating with more spectacular temples and the Royal Palace. The traffic was a nightmare but the tuk-tuk rides were an alternative means of transport and an experience tourists' thought amazing. Violet felt immediately at home in Bangkok, more than she had in Kuala Lumpur. The language was not a problem as many of the assistants in the shops spoke English.

The hotel informed them that there was a large Music school in a residential area called Sukhumvit. An appointment was made and Violet had her CV with her in case there was a post available. After a meeting with the Directors and the staff, Violet viewed the facilities. The School opened from Wednesday to Sunday from midday until seven in the evening and the students were all ages from four-year-olds to adults. The Directors were welcoming and inspected her CV and concert programmes. The outcome was an offer to become the Western Music Advisor to the Music school.

Violet was excited at the thought of working in Thailand but said she would give it serious consideration and let them know when she returned to England.

'I can't believe I have the offer of a post in Bangkok when I came out to find one in Malaysia.'

'It would be very exciting and give you an opportunity to perform as well,' replied Leonard.

The return flight to KL affected Leonard's damaged left ear and he was airsick. At the airport he needed a wheelchair and flying home to UK the next day was out of the question. David arranged a doctor to visit Leonard at the hotel and another week of rest was advised. After several difficult discussions with the insurance company Violet managed to stay with him.

She spent the time swimming, enjoying extra sightseeing and relaxing. Violet organised transport from Heathrow airport and saw Leonard settled in his apartment, before returning to Sunhaven.

'Am I going to work in Bangkok?' wondered Violet. 'What will I do with Sunhaven?'

There were numerous aspects to consider, not the least being her pupils. The original reason for going abroad was to finish her relationship with Leonard and have a new work experience but to her astonishment Leonard suggested joining her in Thailand if she decided to work there.

'I can take early retirement and find a teaching post in Bangkok.'

'Your pension might be reduced and there is no guarantee of a teaching post in Bangkok,' replied Violet.

This plan was not to Violet's liking but his insistence that he loved her and did not want to lose her, softened Violet's attitude. She considered a companion in a foreign country might be an advantage. Their previous trips to Switzerland and Paris had been so enjoyable, perhaps this one would be the same. Also if Leonard failed to find work in Bangkok he would return to England.

'That is a long way to travel. Is there anywhere in Europe you could teach?' asked Joan. 'What will you do with Sunhaven? It is so ideal for your piano teaching and performing, especially with the new extension. I thought how spacious and comfortable it is now, and the garden is beautiful.'

The autumn term started with many of her best pupils leaving for Music Colleges and universities. *Maybe it is a good time to work abroad* thought Violet.

It was a difficult decision but at half-term she decided. Notice was given to all the pupils and alternative music teachers were found where necessary.

Five of her adult pupils had qualified with diplomas so there was a choice of teachers.

Violet had several coffee mornings informing her friends of the move to Bangkok. Her mother was horrified and upset. Bangkok could have been on another planet as far as she was concerned. It was not a known holiday venue and no one knew the language. She could not imagine anyone else living in Sunhaven so arranged for an estate agent to sell it. There was a glowing report about the garden describing it 'as a miniature stately home'. 'A slight exaggeration,' said Violet to her neighbour, laughingly. 'But I have spent a lot of time landscaping it. Now the bungalow and garden are finished maybe it is time to move on to new territory.'

'We will miss you very much,' said the neighbour.

There had been an incident with Greta before Violet had Tristan put down. On one of the horse riding days Greta and Luigi looked after Tristan but on her return Violet found her engagement ring missing from the bedroom. It transpired that Greta had taken it to pawn as Luigi kept her short of money.

He related the incident to Violet but she did not know whether to accuse Greta of theft or claim on the insurance for loss of property. The ring had been one of pearls and garnet from Henry and its personal value was irreplaceable. Eventually Violet did nothing but kept her distance from Greta. Luigi was very sorry Violet was going abroad and the daughter cried when Violet told her she was going away during one of their teas together.

Christmas came with the traditional concert for the pupils. They all prepared a solo and Violet prepared meringues, cupcakes and orange squash for the younger ones as well as fruitcake and tea for the older pupils.

As it was the last concert many of the pupils brought presents saying how much she would be missed. Ryan was devastated and pleaded with her to change her mind and stay at Sunhaven, and the farewell lunch with her adult pupils was very emotional for Violet.

Storage was arranged for all her belongings but her car was going to the sister of one of Violet's pupils. Some of her friends thought she was having a mid-life crisis but with the flight booked, the anticipation of a new life filled Violet with excitement. Leonard had managed to organise his early retirement but decided to keep his flat and arranged for a neighbour to keep an eye on it. He was not on good terms with his wife yet again but she was glad Violet was going to Thailand. Leonard had managed to book a seat on the same flight which pleased Violet. Considering her original plan was to end the relationship completely, she began to think that just the two of them in a foreign country might stabilise it.

Part 4
Thailand

Chapter 17

A car met them at the airport and after checking-in at the hotel, they were driven to the Music School. Leonard was entertained by a beautiful Thai secretary while Violet discussed the teaching hours and her expected agenda. There were numerous teaching rooms and a small recital room. The whole building was air conditioned and the staff seemed to prefer a cool temperature. In addition to individual lessons there were classes for beginners and Violet was surprised when she was informed that the School had several hundred pupils.

Violet was allotted pupils with potential in addition to supervising the teaching staff. Due to their slim figures the female teachers looked very young but some were married with children. They wore very elegant clothes and spoke perfect English, so Violet had no problem with communication.

As a courtesy she decided to take Thai lessons specialising in words relating to musical explanations. Leonard was also learning the Thai language but his search for a teaching position had met with negative results.

Their apartment was spacious but noisy so Violet had difficulty in sleeping at night.

'Can we find a quiet apartment or house to rent, Leonard? I am so tired.' The days were busy with teaching, supervising and practising for concerts and adjusting to the travelling in the city in the heat. The apartment was a bus ride from the Music School and often Violet took a tuk-tuk.

They had a daily cleaner who did some cooking but they ate mostly at restaurants as the Thai food was not wholly to their taste.

Violet had two days free every week and a visit to the British Embassy resulted in a Bridge evening. One of the Embassy staff, Nona, was also a piano teacher. She had spent many years in London working for the BBC and still kept in touch with friends in UK.

'I'll introduce you to some of the well known piano teachers outside the Music School. They have their own studios or teach at the universities. You will find some are competitive but with your expertise and concert performances you will be in demand,' said Nona.

Violet had given three performances during the first six months including one concert with an English cellist. The Ambassador and his wife were very welcoming and invited Violet to give a performance at the Embassy.

'I need a rest,' said Violet to Leonard. 'Can we have a week in a hotel by the sea?'

The Music School granted her two weeks' vacation and Nona suggested Hua Hin as a venue. They hired a car and enjoyed swimming, relaxing by the pool, a little sightseeing, and eating continental food.

'This is what I needed,' said Violet. 'I will be ready for anything when we return to Bangkok.'

On their return Leonard found a letter asking him for an interview at an International school. It was an hour's journey from the apartment but the post included accommodation.

'Will you live there if they offer you the position?' enquired Violet.

'I can still see you when you finish teaching at weekends and also on your free days,' replied Leonard.

Leonard was offered the teaching position so Violet now had to find an apartment for just herself. Eventually one of the teachers found a spacious apartment with a swimming pool in the courtyard.

The Music School arranged for a piano to be delivered and Violet finally settled in with some new furnishings. She had a cook, a cleaning lady and a chauffeur to drive her to work, so her new life had at last become truly enjoyable.

Her work permit had to be renewed every three months so Violet visited Penang and Singapore for an overnight stay. She also had to visit the Education Department to explain why she was working in Thailand. She was expecting the Music School to provide a work permit but they seemed to delay giving her legal status.

The most exciting aspect to her teaching schedule was the piano tuition for the Royal children. Their arrival was heralded by police motor bikes with a security van behind the Royal limousine. There was always an armed guard outside her teaching room so the children were safe. The eldest boy would relate his foreign travels with his father and although there was a lack of piano practice between lessons he was a charming boy to teach.

Violet was asked to prepare a concert in the presence of a first cousin to King Rama VI. She arranged a programme with both teachers and pupils performing and the finale would be her own solos. The Princess would be presented with a bouquet by Violet on one knee, so there were numerous rehearsals with every detail being addressed. Violet visited a tailor for much of her wardrobe so she had a special dress made for the occasion in royal blue lace.

'That is beautiful,' said Leonard admiringly. 'I'll take some photos of you sat at the piano.'

It was a great success so the Directors took Violet to an expensive Thai restaurant to celebrate. She was developing a taste for Thai cuisine so tried several new dishes.

The first Christmas in Bangkok was a complete surprise for Violet. English carols were played in the stores and floodlit decorations festooned the hotels. Hearing 'Hark the herald Angels sing' made her feel homesick and tearful. Even the trees were decorated with coloured lights. She had not expected a Buddhist country to celebrate a Western Christmas or to give presents. Violet and Leonard were invited to a Christmas party for the Royal children. Father Christmas arrived in a sledge pulled by two ponies and the children were entertained by the most popular vocal group in Thailand. Violet felt very honoured to be invited.

The letters from home arrived regularly. Violet suggested a visit to Bangkok by her sister and mother for New Year.

'We can do some shopping as well as sightseeing,' said Violet. 'I'll arrange the hotel and also a few days in Pattaya.'

Her mother was delighted to see Violet and that she was happy working in Bangkok. After all the main sights in Bangkok they arrived at Pattaya to celebrate the New Year. One morning an elephant and her calf were paraded around the grounds of the hotel. Her sister was very nervous but

Violet had no fear of the magnificent animals. She had visited a working group in the jungle where they carried logs and Violet rode on one of the females sitting behind the enormous ears. Its trunk explored her neck and shoulders before she climbed up on its bent knee.

'They are quite gentle and will not hurt you,' Violet told her sister. The calf had put its small trunk on Violet's breasts and one of the other hotel guests said with a laugh, 'Perhaps it is looking for some milk.'

'Leonard tells me you are not serious about him,' said Donna.

'He is the one not making any serious plans for us,' replied Violet. 'We should be living together but he has made no effort to find a house. He did come to Thailand with you so he must have some serious intentions.'

'I think he is seeing a Thai girl and taking her out to dinners. He might even have had sex with her. I still can't trust him and if he loves me he has to be faithful.'

When her mother and sister left for home Violet felt she needed something to cheer her up so a trip was planned to visit Chiang-mai in the north. The festivals were numerous in Thailand and Songran was the major celebration in spring. It was a three day water festival when the people showed respect for monks and elders by sprinkling water over their hands.

Some young boys behaved badly and threw canal water over tourists. Violet saw one visitor being soaked but she escaped with wet sandals and handbag. She was staying at a luxury hotel and enjoyed their traditional Khao Chai with mango sticky rice for dinner.

After a few days Violet returned by train overnight. It was quite an experience as the Thai passengers cooked on the train and all the rubbish was just thrown out on to the railway lines. There was a lot of noise during the night so she slept only a few hours and although it had been an interesting trip, Violet was glad to return to her apartment in Bangkok.

One of the other important Festivals was in November. Nona had arranged for Violet and Leonard to witness the proceedings at a hotel on the river. Loy Kratong celebrated the Goddess of Water whereby lotus shaped vessels, decorated with candles, floated down the river or on a lake. If the candle stayed alight until it was out of sight the person would have a year of good luck. Violet thought it was quite beautiful watching all the lighted candles floating down the river.

'We'll have dinner, then watch the classical Thai dancers,' said Nona. The slim, beautiful Thai girls were stunning to watch in their exquisite silk costumes and Violet bought some tape recordings of the music.

Violet taught a beautiful Thai woman who had been a model. She was now a millionaire and ran her own business. Although she had aperfect figure, Suna wanted larger breasts and a fuller more Western bottom. To Violet's amazement she underwent plastic surgery.

'Do you think I look more shapely?' she asked Violet.

'I think you were beautiful before but you certainly have more curves now,' she replied, laughing.

Suna had divorced her Chinese husband and had built a magnificent house in Bangkok. The Steinway grand piano was positioned in the entrance hall with a sweeping staircase to the bedrooms. Her own bedroom was ensuite on two levels with a walk-in dressing room. The porcelain bathroom had gold taps and a shell shaped hand basin. The only drawback to her home were the two untrained dogs. The pugs had replaced her previous Afghan hounds who were toilet trained and slept in their kennel. But the pug puppies performed their toilet needs on the furniture. The poor maids had to constantly clean up after them.

'Suna, you must train these dogs. It is disgusting to have them relieving themselves indoors. The maids should take them into the garden each morning and then tap their noses if they perform in the house.'

The maids were delighted and relieved at Violet's suggestion but she never discovered whether the dogs were trained before Violet left Bangkok.

Chapter 18

The following year progressed without any problems except the absence of a work permit. Violet had been asked to teach at the University but there was no question of her leaving the Music School as it provided all the musical opportunities that she wanted. It was suggested by one of the teachers that she could have her own studio as well as teaching at the Music School but that would have involved finding a house and not leave her enough time to practise for concerts.

The next major event was organising a concert where all the children performed. Violet composed a piano trio for the Royal children and selected the complete programme. The main guest was the Crown Prince but there would also be military personnel, wealthy parents and the families of the teachers. The event was held in a hotel ballroom so security had to be arranged in addition to a grand piano being installed and tuned. The stage was decorated with large displays of flowers and all the children had special outfits made for the occasion.

'I was very nervous,' Violet told Nona. 'After the performance, I was introduced to the Crown Prince and to my shame I forgot to curtsey. He waited but I expected him to speak first. I just froze and so he walked past me to the waiting limousine and police escort.'

'I expect he realised you were nervous,' consoled Nona. 'It was such a special event.'

To her delight a few months later Violet was formally introduced to the Crown Prince at his home and presented with a gold pen. She remembered to curtsey and walk backwards as she left the room.

'We are having a visit from Jane Bastien next month,' said one of the Directors.

'I can organise an informal concert with the young pupils,' replied Violet. The Music School and piano teachers worldwide used the Bastien books for tuition. They covered theory, the technique and performance and were Invaluable and the illustrations entertained very young pupils.

Violet had never met either James or Jane Bastien but she had used the Piano books in her own teaching with excellent results and enjoyment from the students.

'It will be such a pleasure to meet her and talk about her publications.' Violet was amazed at the energy and enthusiasm of Jane when they met and talked about teaching the piano. She finally departed for Hong Kong and Violet felt sad at her departure.

Violet was enjoying a social life with the teachers and friends at the Embassy. Several of the teachers had gained a Master's Degree in the United States and as Violet was considering a further qualification, she thought a year back in the UK to study for another degree would be beneficial for her career.

'I am thinking about returning to England to study for a Master's Degree,' she told Leonard.

'If the music school does not provide a work permit I might not return to Bangkok.'

'What about us?' asked Leonard.

'Well, we have not been living together and you seem to be enjoying other activities without me. Are you having a relationship with one of the teachers?'

'Of course not, I took Siri for a meal when you were teaching, but nothing else.'

Violet was not convinced as Leonard had lied so many times before about having other affairs. The Directors of the Music School were upset about her leaving Bangkok but promised a work permit when she returned from her Degree course.

It was a major operation packing all her belongings into crates and boxes. There was a complete dinner service, pieces of furniture, her concert and Thai wardrobe, and gifts and souvenirs. Violet planned to travel with just one suitcase and all the rest would return to England by ship.

There was a farewell dinner and the staff were very tearful at her departure, but she would keep in touch with a few by post and telephone. Her journey back to UK was via India. Violet had wanted to visit India and Cambodia while living in Thailand but her musical commitments had not allowed time. Also there was fighting in Cambodia and the Embassy advised visits only on days when the fighting had ceased temporarily.

Violet arrived in Delhi and a taxi took her to the hotel. It was certainly not de luxe.

'Have you another room available? There is a wide gap above the door so anyone can look in and I might be undressing,' she complained to the manager.

'Very busy, madam, no other room available.'

Violet contemplated moving to another hotel but all the staff spoke English and the restaurant served an excellent selection of Asian and continental food.

On the first day Violet joined a tour of Delhi, visiting the memorial to Gandhi and Humayun's tomb – a sixteenth-century Mughal garden-tomb. The next day was a visit to old Delhi to see the Red Fort, or Lal Qila, on the banks of the Yamuna river. Violet was impressed with the sandstone walls that glowed in the sunshine. She took photos of Jama Masjid, India's largest mosque as well as the red Fort.

Her guide book told her that the urban plan for Delhi was drawn up by Sir Edwin Lutyens in the early twentieth century. He was an architect with a deep knowledge of imperial grandeur and so included monumental symbols of the British Empire. The Viceroy's house was a vast palace with 340 rooms, a central dome and acres of manicured gardens.

After a day of relaxing by the pool and some shopping Violet booked a trip to Jaipur. The pink capital of Rajasthan was noisy but colourful and exciting.

She visited the Moon Palace, the residence of the former ruling family. It was a fusion of Hindu and Mughal styles with arches, marble columns and decorative elephants.

The highlight was Wawa Mahal that had been built for the ladies of the harem. The multiple jali screens were designed to catch the breeze so it was called "Palace of the Winds".

The days were passing quickly and there were still two famous places to visit. Fatehpur Sikri was a city built by the emperor Akbar in the seventeenth century. Violet remembered being told when she lived in London that her

Akbar was named after an emperor so now in India she had to see the deserted city.

Apparently a holy man, in a village called Sikri, foretold the birth of three sons for the childless emperor. When the prophecy became a reality Fatehpur, meaning "town of victory", was added to the village name by the emperor. Violet wondered whether her Akbar was now married and still living in London.

Agra was to be the final place to visit. The Taj Mahal was as breathtaking as Violet had hoped. Built by Shah Jahan for his favourite wife, Mumtaz Mahal, it is a monument to love.

Violet gazed at the shimmering white marble reflected in the water channel and her thoughts were of Henry. She thought of the memorial to him if she had the wealth of a maharajah and decided probably a Music Academy would be the most fitting establishment. Violet often wondered at her love for Henry especially due to their age difference, but she had read recently about Cary Grant and his final marriage to a young girl of just 30 years. He apparently had several serious relationships including four earlier marriages, but at 77 years he finally found the love of his life.

They only had five years together before he died and Violet thought how similar Cary Grant and Henry were, even to the period of being married to the love of their lives.

The airport was chaotic as the conveyor belt for the luggage had broken down. Violet saw her suitcase thrown on to a trolley and was glad it only contained clothes with nothing breakable. Her souvenirs were in her hand luggage and all the china and glass items had been packed in the crates to be sent by ship. She was relieved when the plane landed at Heathrow airport. Violet had loved living in Thailand, and the musical activities had been exciting as well as making new friends but she only felt truly at home when in England.

Part 5
Berkshire & Beech Tree

Chapter 19

Violet arrived at her mother's flat to a delicious English roast dinner.

'I have missed this food in Bangkok,' said Violet. 'Some of the hotels had a comprehensive restaurant, but their roast dinners were never like home.'

'I am so glad you are back in England. Have you arranged storage for your boxes from Thailand? There is no room here unfortunately as I don't have a garage.'

'All my belongings are being delivered to my original storage company. I can just collect winter clothes when I need them.'

There had been a choice of York or Reading for the Master's Degree. Violet had been offered a place at both universities but as Evelyn's husband was now a bursar at Reading University and it was nearer to her mother, Reading was selected.

Violet had bought a small car as she needed to be mobile. Her accommodation was a room in one of the Halls of residence and her Greek neighbours were very friendly but noisy, holding late drinking sessions until after midnight. As Violet needed her sleep with hours of piano practice in addition to the studies for her thesis, she moved to a rented room in a private house. It was owned by a headmaster and his family. The room was spacious with cooking facilities and a private en suite. The area outside her room was a utility area and one morning as she staggered half asleep to the toilet Violet met a man in overalls.

'Good morning to you,' he said with a smile. 'Hope I didn't wake you but I need to finish the work as soon as possible.'

It transpired the builder was constructing some units and installing extra plumbing. Little did she know what the future had in store for the two of them.

The professor in charge of the Music department was a past pupil of Fanny Waterman so there was a personal connection. He was an exceptional pianist and musician so Violet was delighted she had chosen Reading University.

'It is very demanding as I have to give seminars and two public recitals,' explained Violet.

'But it is what you want to achieve,' replied Evelyn. 'The research in the Oxford archives for your thesis sounds fascinating.'

Violet spent most evenings with Evelyn and her husband in their University apartment. She could also use their washing machine for her clothes. Philip was an excellent cook so there was always a delicious dinner followed by coffee and chocolates.

'What would I do without you two!' said Violet in appreciation. Their daughter was married and the son was finishing a degree in Manchester. The close friendship with Evelyn had just continued on their return to the UK and they still discussed any personal problems.

Violet enjoyed the friendship of the other students on the Master's Degree course although it was a small group. One of them was a member of the aristocracy and laughed when called "her Ladyship". Sylvia was a talented musician and Violet envied her compositions and her ability to play several instruments.

'You know the professor has a reputation for seducing first year students,' remarked Sylvia.

'I know, he shows concern and affection for me every time we are together,' answered Violet. 'But the extra evening sessions are purely to discuss my thesis.'

During the final weeks in the summer Violet looked after the professor's two cats. She had the use of his house and could entertain any friends.

The degree was duly passed with distinction and Violet returned to Devon to stay with her mother until she made a decision about her future musical career. The atmosphere was not as friendly as before as one of the scrabble groups had warned her mother about Violet taking over the flat and putting her in a care home. The whole idea was ludicrous as Violet had two choices in relation to where she would be living. Either a return to Thailand or a piano tutor position in a Music College in UK. There had been several offer to teach the piano but no position that was full-time.

'I need a full-time position if I stay in UK to obtain a mortgage. Wherever I am working I want a home of my own,' explained Violet. 'I have been looking in the Educational Supplement but there is only school music teachers advertised, nothing in Music Colleges.'

'Just keep looking. Perhaps your professor at Reading University could help,' replied her mother.

The need for some financial income forced Violet to take a teaching post in Wiltshire.

'It will give me time to decide my future and I will be renting a room near the school,' she informed her mother.

Having been an independent musician for twenty five years Violet found the class teaching and routine in the school a miserable experience. The salary and short hours made it bearable.

'Thank goodness it is only for two terms,' she told Evelyn.

The rented room was in a house owned by a divorced woman who managed the main office of a national refrigeration company. Lorna was very attractive and had a 12-year-old daughter who lived most of the time with her grandparents. When Lorna stayed in the house there was often a visit from her regular boyfriend. His sleep-over was particularly noisy and left nothing to anyone's imagination.

Another girl was renting the third bedroom and after a few weeks became a good friend of Violet. Alice was working for a large company that had its main office in Germany. She loved her job but it was very demanding.

'I could do with more sleep,' complained Alice. 'Did you hear them last night?'

'Yes, but at least it is only a few nights,' replied Violet.

The daughter was delightful and had a passion for "Phantom of the Opera" by Andrew Lloyd Webber and Violet told her about meeting his father at the Royal College of Music where he was a professor.

One disturbing situation occurred when Violet had been taking her nightly bath. A wooden knot in the door had fallen out leaving a hole, so anyone could look into the bathroom.

Unknown to Violet and Alice, the boyfriend had been spying on them during their ablutions.

'Do we tell Lorna what her boyfriend has been doing?' asked Alice.

'If we hang our dressing gowns over the hole, he won't be able to look in. At least we have the house to ourselves most of the time,' replied Violet.

They decided to keep quiet and not mention the problem to Lorna. A lump of cotton wool was also pushed into the hole.

'Would you be interested in becoming Head of the Music Department?' asked the Headmaster.

'Goodness, I will have to think about that!' replied Violet. She was astonished at the offer but her aim was to perform and teach in a Music College. The only position that offered piano teaching entailed being a Housemistress to the sixth form in a boarding school. There would be some opportunity for performing and Violet would have her own flat. The salary was excellent and enabled her to obtain a mortgage. There was a substantial amount from the sale of Sunhaven but Violet had bought a new Steinway grand piano and a car so she required additional funds to buy a house.

Violet had decided not to return to Thailand so accepted the boarding school position and started a search for a property while staying with Evelyn and her husband, Philip, at Reading University.

'I need to find a house before the autumn term begins,' said Violet. 'There is one south of the M4 that is detached and with some alterations, can accommodate my Steinway.'

Philip gave it a detailed inspection as he was good at detecting any building problems.

'You could knock that wall down and make a large room for your piano and the smaller room could be your living room. There is room for a separate utility area if you have a wall erected at the end of the large room. You can stay with us until the house is ready,' offered Philip.

The purchase went smoothly as Violet was a cash buyer. The house was called Beechtree as it had a weeping beech tree in the garden.

'I think I might ask that builder I met when I was renting a room here,' said Violet. 'He seemed very efficient and at least I know the quality of his work. Can you start immediately?' asked Violet, after arranging an inspection of the house.

'No problem, ma'am,' replied Ross, the builder.

The changes in the house started with the wall being removed, then several doors were blocked, radiators moved and new windows installed.

'I think I can move in before Christmas,' said Violet.

Carpets were laid, furniture delivered from storage and the Steinway piano moved into the new room two weeks before Christmas Eve. Although Violet was excited at having a new home, she missed the warm, sunny weather in Thailand. She also wondered what Leonard was doing as he had decided to stay in Bangkok. There would be no shortage of Thai girls to be entertained or seduced, but he was still faced with the decision of divorce from his wife. 'Some of my clothes and bedding are missing,' complained Violet. 'All my skiing clothes are gone and the bedding was new.'

'You can claim on your insurance,' replied Philip.

When Violet made a list of the items it reached over a thousand pounds in value. The storage warehouse had been broken into and her boxes had been opened with the contents removed. Many of the clothes could not be replaced and Violet was close to tears. All the other arrangements to move into the house had gone smoothly so this was a real blow.

'We'll have a mega shopping expedition,' said Evelyn. 'It will be enjoyable to choose bedding for your new double bed as well as some elegant winter outfits.'

Chapter 20

Violet no longer used her performing name that had been adopted while she was married to Henry. As her talent had been inherited from her grandmother Violet inserted her grandmother's married name to form a hyphened surname for herself. During the period after World War 2 it was fashionable for artists to have a double-barrelled name. At the Music School in Bangkok and now in the boarding school she was known as Mrs Fullerton.

The duties were varied but the responsibility for the girls was day and night. There was time for piano practice in the music wing so Violet tried to maintain a regular routine. Teaching titled and wealthy girls was a complete contrast to the previous school but a fascinating experience.

'The Royal family connection is not daunting after my involvement in Bangkok,' said Violet to Evelyn. 'But their social life entails buying designer clothes, and being seen at well known events like Henley Regatta and Wimbledon Tennis tournament. They are no longer presented at court to the Queen as debutantes but Queen Charlotte's Ball is still an important occasion for them.'

'Have you met any famous parents?' enquired Evelyn.

'Oh yes, and I often entertain them in my flat to discuss their daughters.' For some staff their whole existence revolved around the school and the girls but Violet wanted to resume her Bridge as well as finding a male companion when she was at home.

'I have been using a dating agency and it is so entertaining,' she confessed to Evelyn. 'I meet them at the V & A Museum in London for lunch or tea.

Sometimes we do a little sightseeing or if we are interested in each other, we sit and chat.'

'Have you met anyone you fancy?' asked Evelyn.

'Well, one has a house in France and is a professional musician and one other works for the Thames Water Board. Raymond – the Waterman, as I call him – is my age, so we are making a few dates. He also lives just a few miles from the boarding school, so meeting will be quite easy.'

The time spent with Raymond developed into a regular relationship and the sixth form girls cheered when he collected Violet in his sports car.

Raymond kept physically very fit by running marathons and mountain climbing. 'How about a trip to Snowdonia,' he enquired. 'We can stay for a few nights and you can learn to climb.'

'Where will we stay? Have you booked a hotel?'

'There are community camping huts that are spacious and have cooking facilities.'

Violet thought the accommodation arrangements sounded very basic, and she was correct. On arrival at the camp site another climber cooked a meal that they shared as there was plenty. But when Violet saw the sleeping area she was horrified. It was a wooden bench where each climber laid down in their sleeping bag next to each other.

'I'll sleep at the end against the wall and you can lie between me and the other person,' she informed Raymond.

To her surprise Violet did manage to have several hours of sleep. The morning ablutions were limited, and therefore brief, before setting off with climbing gear. The second day Violet managed a solo climb and abseiled down safely.

'You have done really well considering you are afraid of heights,' said Raymond. 'We'll climb higher tomorrow.'

The next day when they reached the top, Violet was amazed to see and hear jet planes flying below through the valley.

Then disaster struck. Raymond damaged his back so Violet had to pack all the climbing gear in the car and drive him to the Radcliffe hospital in Oxford. 'It was a nightmare!!! He screamed everytime a nurse touched him and they gave him an injection to calm him down,' complained Violet.

'What was the damage?' asked Evelyn.

'It was a slipped disc and he has to have total rest for several weeks. I can do a few things like shopping and cooking meals for the freezer, but I need to be back at the house.'

Ross had been working in the house putting up shelves, hanging mirrors and pictures. He had installed a new hi-fi unit and as a qualified gas engineer had connected her new cooker. Ross moved large pieces of furniture in addition to connecting the new light fittings.

Violet had kept in touch with Alice and when she needed to rent a room near her boyfriend's home, Violet suggested Beechtree. Alice moved in with Ken and while Violet was away at the boarding school they kept the house in perfect condition as well as cutting the lawns. For Violet It was an excellent arrangement as it provided security while she was away and companionship during the vacations.

The reliance on Ross for doing jobs in the house continued but he was becoming more than a builder to Violet. She realised how pleased she was to see him and that an attraction was developing. As well as Sinatra and Ella Fitzgerald Violet enjoyed Diana Ross, especially her CD called 'The Force behind the Power' but it was not just the name that reminded her of her builder.

Raymond had duly recovered and suggested a holiday in the Canary Islands. 'We can stay in Tenerife and climb Mount Teide,' he said. 'It would be very gentle with no serious rock climbing.'

They went for a week over the New Year celebrations and although the days were warm it became cold during the nights.

'There is snow at the top of Mount Teide but there are stunning views and the sun will be warm.' Violet found the climb tiring but the views were well worth the effort.

They hired a car for some sightseeing and the week passed very quickly. Violet had enjoyed the trip but she found Raymond somewhat conceited. Their relationship was very different from the one with Leonard when she had shared music and Bridge. Although Leonard loved sailing, he was not a keen sportsman like Raymond and certainly never boasted about his achievements. Violet was now thinking more about her builder than her present boyfriend.

Evelyn had remarked on all the extra jobs Ross did for free. 'He obviously is attracted to you and enjoys your company.'

'I need another wall unit for my vinyl recordings, Ross. Where is the best place?' asked Violet. As she watched him fix the unit, she thought how handsome he was and had an urge to kiss him.

'Can I pay in kind?' asked Violet with a laugh and kissed him firmly on the mouth. His response was more than she had even imagined.

'I'll call to see you when you have your next free day.' Ross held her close, kissing her mouth repeatedly, before leaving.

Violet felt her heart racing in the same way as when she met Henry. Was this going to be another fraught love affair with a married man? Ross arrived at the house early on her next free day and stayed for lunch. Within a few weeks he became her lover.

'I have stopped seeing Raymond and I think he was relieved. It was certainly not a love affair but suited us both socially and met our physical needs.'

'You know my family prevent me from having any serious future plans with you,' said Ross.

The need to see each other and the passion in their lovemaking would appear to an outsider as very serious. Violet often telephoned from her flat to arrange a meeting time. 'It's me,' she said.

'Hello, you,' Ross replied. 'I can be with you tomorrow before you leave for the Bridge Club.'

Because Ross had seen her at her worst in the morning coming out of the rented room, Violet felt completely at ease with him. She woke in the mornings thinking about him and memories of their time together was the last thought at night.

Apart from house renovations, Ross was willing to help in the garden. He lowered one of the long hedges and installed a hammock that Violet had brought back from Thailand. A large pond had been dug in the centre of the garden and after lining it with butyl, Ross helped Violet lay the paving stones that provided a solid edging and path. The earth from the pond became a rockery and the twenty two fish Violet had inherited from the previous owners enjoyed their new home.

Over the years the garden became a major hobby with changing plants, new shrubs and an additional small pond for a fish nursery. One hazard was the number of frogs each spring. They produced thousands of tadpoles so Violet collected the frogs in a bucket and took them to a nearby river.

'I feel sorry for the females,' said Violet. 'They have to tolerate being attached to the mating males for days.'

'Lucky males,' laughed Ross. 'We have to keep an eye on the clock when we make love.'

Their time together was always hours and Violet longed to spend a day with him. 'Why do I fall in love with married men?' she moaned to herself.

When Violet moved into Beechtree she had no thoughts of it being a long term home or creating a garden that would give her so much joy. Each year there were changes and new delights.

Alice and Ken had moved to a house but a surprise telephone call produced a new lodger. A former pupil of Violet had qualified with a music degree and had a teaching position in a school less than 20 miles away. She had discovered where Violet lived and contacted her by telephone,

147

wanting to meet after several years. The need for accommodation near the school led to Angie renting the spare room at Beechtree. Violet was delighted to see her again and have a familiar tenant.

'Are you still performing?' asked Angie.

'Most of the time is spent teaching the piano and accompanying the choir and examination candidates. But I did give a public performance of The Snowman with the local Symphony orchestra.'

'Your builder is very handsome. I can see why you fell for him!' said Angie.

'But he is married so unavailable,' replied Violet. 'We only ever have a few hours together. He calls in for coffee some mornings and we spend an afternoon on my free days. It would be so good to have a whole day, we enjoy being together so much, apart from the sexual aspect.'

Chapter 21

The original plan by Violet was to stay at the boarding school for one year, but there was real affection between her and the girls in the sixth form so she stayed for another year. Her piano teaching had produced excellent results and the parents were very appreciative so the years passed.

Now Violet was in her fourth year but her young assistant was causing a problem.

'She is wearing our designer jeans and tops,' complained one of the girls. 'They are taken from the laundry room.'

Violet reported the details to the Bursar and he suggested inspecting her cottage. They found the items reported by the girls and the assistant was asked to leave at the end of the summer term.

The situation was obviously discussed by the parents of the sixth form girls in Violet's flat. To her amazement the Headmistress reprimanded Violet for being disloyal to the school. She was subjected to an inquest by the Bursar, the Headmistress and two other housemistresses accusing her of total disloyalty to the school and its reputation.

'It is probably due to jealousy,' said Evelyn, on being told of the situation. 'You are musically talented, have a social life outside the school and the girls adore you.'

Violet eventually took recourse to a solicitor about defamation of character who advised taking the Headmistress to court.

'I will take you to court if necessary and tomorrow you will receive two letters – one from my solicitor and the other my resignation,' she informed the Headmistress.

There was a music position at a boarding school nearer to the house and Violet had accepted starting in the New Year.

'The good news is that I will be at home more often,' said Violet.

'So, I can see you more than once a week during the term,' replied Ross. 'Is the salary the same?'

'Only a little less but I can take private pupils at home.'

It was a sad final term with the sixth form girls but the new assistant housemistress had formed an excellent relationship with them. She was young, attractive and had a sense of humour. Violet liked her immediately. They went shopping, had supper together and shared personal details.

The term was busy with several piano pupils taking Associated Board examinations and Violet was also performing "The Snowman" with the local Symphony orchestra.

There was a formal apology from the Headmistress and she asked Violet to read the lesson at the Christmas Carol Service. It was an important event with the parents and full church attendance.

'You are wanted in the main hall,' said the Head of Music. 'Am I in more trouble?' asked Violet.

To her astonishment the whole school was assembled with no staff. 'We want you to know how much we will miss you,

Mrs Fullerton,' said the Head girl. 'Will you accept these gifts as a thank you for all you have done for us.'

Violet felt tears coming but swallowed to control the emotion. They all sang 'For she's a jolly good fellow and so say all of us.' The loud cheering and clapping was heard in the nearby staff room and eventually the Head of Music told the staff that the girls were giving a loving farewell to their favourite housemistress. Violet said her farewells to the staff and drove to Devon to spend Christmas with her mother.

New Year was celebrated with Evelyn and Philip at their University flat. The week before term commenced Violet enjoyed her new Steinway piano, revising past recital programmes and memorising new repertoire. In addition to enjoying Beechtree, Ross paid a brief visit to tell her how much he had missed her over the Christmas and New Year celebrations.

'I imagined holding you close on Christmas Day and ached for your mouth on mine. Seeing you more often this year will be wonderful.'

'I think I can find a few more jobs for you,' laughed Violet.

There was a decision to be made regarding the Laser. Sailing on an inland lake did not give the same enjoyment or excitement as sailing at sea. Violet had continued her horse riding at the local stables but it was expensive. Also unless clients were competing in events, they were given slow, ageing horses to ride. Trotting around country lanes and across adjoining fields did not compare with galloping across Dartmoor.

Compensation for selling her boat and abandoning horse riding were visits to London for recitals and concerts. Violet saw famous pianists, conductors and orchestras at the Festival Hall and Albert Hall. Returning to the Proms reminded her of the students days when she queued for a seat in the Promenade. Many of the programmes also reminded Violet of Henry and performing in Bangkok.

The new boarding school had fewer pupils than the previous one but many of the girls had the same problems. Often their parents were abroad so birthdays were not celebrated and vacations were spent with grandparents.

The lack of attention or affection for some of the girls caused serious emotional disorders whereby they would cut themselves or become anorexic. Violet realised how important the family was to young children and their need to feel loved. No amount of wealth compensated for this deficiency. It was the close friendship of the other girls that provided an affectionate birthday celebration if the parents were skiing or sailing in the Caribbean.

The accommodation at the school was a large bed-sitting room with an en suite bathroom. There was a toaster and electric kettle but Violet brought her own microwave oven. The girls frequently wanted toast before going to bed in the dormitories as well as watching some television. The chef and kitchen staff provided delicious lunches, teas and suppers so the girls always had plenty of nutritious food.

The security was strong and with the presence of a member of the Royal family a Chinook helicopter patrolled regularly. Violet enjoyed being a member of the Music Department as it was organised by a young, efficient and talented girl who became a long-term friend. There were few opportunities to perform and Violet struggled to find time to practise. She had taken another piano teaching post to boost her income at a private girls' school. The school had a high level of music making with an orchestra and choir. Violet provided the piano accompaniment for other instruments during examinations and eventually gave piano lessons to the Headmistress.

Ross came to Beechtree frequently and Violet also managed to play Bridge every week.

'I would like a patio door in the lounge,' said Violet, 'but can we install it with the piano in situ?'

'Leave it to your knight in shining overalls,' replied Ross.

He erected a plastic screen and with a building colleague installed the patio doors where there had been just a window.

'You are so good at overcoming building problems,' said Violet as they lay in bed the next afternoon. 'There have been so many difficulties with Beechtree, I cannot imagine anyone else having the ease with which you solved them.'

'Our love seems to be the only unsolvable problem.'

The London visits continued for recitals and concerts, occasionally meeting a past pupil, Terry, for a drink in The Archduke on the South Bank. On one occasion Terry was not in the restaurant or waiting outside the concert hall.

Violet checked again in the Archduke and as it was almost time for the recital to start hurried to the Queen Elizabeth Hall. As she reached the entry doors two tall coloured men tried to snatch her handbag. She had it under her arm with the strap over her shoulder. They pulled at the handbag and then sprayed her with pepper spray and pushed her against the glass doors.

Violet hung onto her handbag so they gave up and hurried away. Shaking with shock and choking from the spray, Violet staggered to the box office saying she had been attacked. The girl just looked at her.

'I have been attacked by two men,' screamed Violet. 'Ring the police!'

She went to the ladies toilet and was sick. As the manager of the QE Hall arrived a police car pulled up. A chair was brought for Violet but she had to sit outside as the spray had impregnated her clothes so that the police kept a few feet away to avoid inhaling the fumes.

The police and manager expressed their concern and suggested Violet should go to a hospital.

'I want to hear the recital,' she complained.

A statement was taken and the police informed her that they would be in touch. She removed her coat for it to be hung in the cloakroom and met Terry in the interval. He was shocked at her attack.

'Do you want to stay over in our house?' asked Terry. 'You can travel back to Beechtree in the morning.'

'No, I want to hear the rest of the recital and then you can walk me to the underground. Maybe a cup of coffee would help to soothe my nerves.'

Her hair still smelled of the spray but the recital calmed her and she stopped shaking.

'I came straight to the QE Hall as it was too late for drinks. We must have just missed each other,' said Terry apologetically. 'Are you sure you will be alright travelling alone on the train from Paddington?'

'I'll be fine. The trains run regularly to Reading and my car is parked outside the station.'

The police contacted her the following week asking Violet to come to London to try to identify the two men. It was impossible as she only remembered they were tall and wore leather coats. When she told Evelyn and Philip they were horrified and made her promise not to travel to London alone. Her concert visits to London on her own stopped but Violet enjoyed a visit to the Proms that summer with one of the peripatetic music staff. They had a picnic in Kensington gardens near the Albert memorial with glasses of wine and she was driven home in their car. Ross had consoled her but she continued to feel nervous for several months. Violet had loved living in London in the 1960s and this Prom visit restored her confidence.

Chapter 22

Weekly visits to the local Bridge Club improved Violet's card skills and she made several close friends. During the vacations she held a Bridge supper evening. The two tables of four players were in separate rooms and after the game had finished a light supper was provided. It was an extremely enjoyable evening and provided a social life for Violet during the holidays.

Her meetings with Ross were becoming less as he was developing a guilty conscience. A week without him was miserable for Violet but she had always understood the relationship would not last indefinitely. Their lovemaking was still very intense and their pleasure at being together had not diminished. 'You should find someone else, Violet. I still love you but it is becoming more difficult for me to see you.'

Ross was a Catholic and Violet wondered if he had been to confession. She hated to see him suffering but the situation was familiar to her, reminding her of Henry and the anguish they had suffered. Perhaps it was time to find an unmarried male companion.

'I think your love affair should end,' said Angie. 'You need to have a male friend to travel with you on holidays who is free. I know Ross is special but there is no future for you both.'

Violet had told Angie about her love for Ross as she had become a very close friend. They shared their experiences whether it was work difficulties or personal problems and having taught Angie when she was a teenager there was also the musical bond between them. On her free days Violet always looked forward to seeing Angie in Beechtree almost as if she was a family member.

'There is a man at the Bridge Club whom I find very attractive. He comes to my Bridge supper evenings but a woman answers the telephone when I make an arrangement so I assume he is married or has a partner,' said Violet. 'You must find out his personal status. Another married man will not do,' pleaded Angie.

William worked for an airline at Heathrow airport so was often absent from the Bridge Club meetings. They both had regular Bridge partners so there was no personal conversation during the interval.

Violet decided to put her love life on hold and when the teaching and duties ended at the boarding school, she spent the summer organising the garden. All the ericas were removed and she created two new borders with an assortment of herbaceous plants. The fish were flourishing with several babies that were removed to the nursery pond.

When Violet bought Beechtree, she discovered there were stables and a sailing club nearby that had added to her enjoyment of owning the house. Although she no longer sailed or went riding there was the proximity of three garden centres and there were numerous country walks to enjoy.

Violet had converted the plastic pond that she had inherited into a bog garden at the base of the rockery. While moving a rock with her foot she felt a sharp pain in her back. The pain increased so all plans for the garden came to a halt. It was a slipped disc and the doctor ordered complete rest for several weeks.

Angie had moved out and was living with her fiancé so Violet asked Evelyn to help with the recovery. Her bed was moved into the snug with the TV as Violet was unable to climb the stairs. Walking was extremely painful so she had to reach the downstairs toilet on her knees. Evelyn cooked her meals and brought them to Beechtree every day in addition to videos for Violet to watch. She became a Clint Eastwood fan and discovered he was a talented pianist as well as an actor/director.

The inflammation in her back lessened during the following month so hydrotherapy was arranged. Evelyn drove her to a local school where there was a heated pool for exercising.

'I cannot believe it is taking so long to heal,' moaned Violet. 'Apparently, I will have a permanent weakness in my back and will need to be careful about lifting anything heavy. Thank goodness it will not prevent me from sitting at the piano.'

She finally went back to part-time piano teaching at the boarding school but it was November before she resumed full-time duties and piano lessons. One of the staff requested piano lessons with a view to taking an Associated Board examination. Catherine was popular with the girls as she showed concern for their difficulties and always had time to listen. She was to become Violet's closest friend.

During the Easter holidays there was a concert at The Anvil in Basingstoke. Angie was in Devon with her parents so Violet decided to invite William to accompany her. He knew many of the popular classics, such the William Tell overture, the New World Symphony and the Grieg piano concerto. He confessed in the interval that he had a problem sitting still and even though his seat was at the end of the row it was an effort to keep still.

There were several dates after the concert including a walk in Windsor Park and a cinema visit. William mentioned his daughter so Violet discovered there was no wife or partner, just his daughter living with him. Clare moved into her own house a few months after Violet began dating William so his only companion was the family golden retriever, Max.

'I had a golden retriever when I lived in Devon,' said Violet. 'He was devoted to me but due to serious ailments had to be put down. I still miss him.'

They took Max for long walks and their meetings were becoming a real source of pleasure for Violet. Her feelings for Ross were still very strong but the future looked bleak for them.

'I am having one of my Bridge evenings next week, can you come?' asked Violet.

'It will be as delightful as always. You make everyone so welcome,' replied William.

The Bridge was followed by a delicious supper and William offered to help clear up the dishes. The other players had left so Violet gave William a brief kiss on the cheek which resulted in a full mouth kiss.

'Would you like to stay the night?' asked Violet softly.

After William departed the next morning Violet questioned her invitation. Had she just wanted a replacement for Ross or was there genuine feeling for William. He had been so kind and thoughtful as well as physically exciting that maybe a more serious relationship would develop.

'I have a new man friend,' Violet told Ross. 'Is he married? Do you have feelings for him?'

'He seems very caring and I am meeting his son and daughter next week. I can't imagine not seeing you but perhaps we can remain just loving friends.'

'That might be difficult as I always feel a physical attraction when we meet.

I hope this guy is genuine and will take care of you. You can always contact me on my mobile if there is a problem.'

'He is divorced but the divorce was amicable and they still have a family reunion for the birthday celebrations of the children.'

The lunch arranged to meet William's grown up children was nerve-racking for Violet.

'I'll just pop into the ladies,' said Violet to William.

'She inspected her appearance but still felt nervous. What if the son and daughter were unfriendly?' she pondered.

'At last, I thought you were never coming out for lunch,' said William, laughing.

Clare and Ward were very welcoming to Violet and seemed pleased their father had a serious relationship. They ordered lunch and talked about their respective careers with Violet's musical career being the main topic.

'Your children are very close to you, William, and were making sure I was a suitable partner.'

'Now you have been vetted you can relax. They were very interested in your performing career although neither of them are musical.'

William and Violet were now acknowledged as a regular couple at the Bridge Club and there was a cheer when they arrived holding hands. They managed to see each other several times a week which included overnight visits when William's shift work permitted.

Chapter 23

'Would you like a holiday in the United States?' asked William. 'My work with the airlines will allow us to travel free except for airport taxes. We can have two weeks in Florida.'

'That will be brilliant. I have never been across the Atlantic. Can you book a hotel?' replied Violet.

Her first flight to America was memorable as a friend of William in the VIP Lounge at Heathrow airport supplied a glass of champagne before they boarded the plane and then their seats were in first class. The breakfast started with more champagne although Violet opted for a Mimosa. She sat in the comfortable seat beside William brimming over with excitement and held his hand as they took off.

The fortnight in Florida was spent swimming, walking and sightseeing in perfect sunny weather.

'Every day is sunny and we can wear beach clothes all the time,' said Violet with delight. 'I will return to UK with a lovely sun tan.'

She enjoyed the shopping and eating out in diners and restaurants. The added enjoyment was driving the hired car. It was strange driving on the opposite side of the road and

Violet had to watch the traffic lights very attentively as they were only red or green.

It was the beginning of world travel for Violet. In the autumn they visited Niagara Falls and Montreal, followed by a spring trip to California. She loved the Universal Studios in Los Angeles, experiencing the sets for well known films. There was a brief visit to Paris before spending the Easter holidays in Florida.

'Do you want to try living together?' asked Violet. 'It would save the driving to each others' houses on our free days. As well as the pleasure of sleeping together every night,' added Violet smiling.

'I would love it,' replied William, 'but you do know I set the alarm for 4.30 in the morning when I am on the early shift. Can you cope with that?'

'We'll try it for a few months and see if it works for us. I haven't lived with anyone for nearly thirty years so keep your house available in case you need to move back,' suggested Violet.

There was a need to move furniture to accommodate William's belongings. A collection of Toby Jugs, books, CD's and his clothes all required a place but with lots of laughter they managed to organise everything.

The second double bedroom became the study with new office furniture for the computer and files. Violet loved coming home to Beechtree to find William waiting for her, frequently making tea as well as cooking dinner for them.

William enjoyed cooking so there was an extensive range of cookery books that provided interesting recipes. The only aspect to their living together that posed a problem for Violet was the lack of quiet times as she needed to have some time in the day without the television, radio or music that William enjoyed even when cooking. A routine was developed eventually that suited both of them so William decided to rent his house to University students.

He employed an agency to oversee the tenants but after several problems that the agency failed to solve, William sold the property.

'You are happier without the worry of tenants and the sale will boost your financial position,' consoled Violet.

'You are correct about my feeling relieved but are you still happy with me living in Beechtree?'

'I love you being here but you might have to wait a while before planning a wedding. I still enjoy being a free woman,' answered Violet.

There was a return visit to Thailand where Violet met with her friends at the Music School and the British Embassy and William was introduced, to the teachers delight.

'He is a joy,' said Nona, 'and obviously is devoted to you.'

Violet and William enjoyed more world travels to The Gambia, China and Washington DC. As they were on "Standby" for the flights there were often long periods waiting at airports but Violet always felt the thrill of arriving at their destination.

Violet had received a telephone call from her sister about their mother having had a brief period of sickness. Donna had driven their mother to her home in the Midlands to supervise her recovery. Violet drove up to visit her mother on Maundy Thursday and she had been diagnosed with a heart problem.

'I have not felt so miserable for years,' complained her mother. 'Apparently there is a heart murmur and I keep fainting.'

'I expect the medication will help and as soon as you feel well enough Donna will drive you back to Devon,' said Violet.

Back home in Beechtree, Violet felt she should have stayed overnight with her sister to spend longer with their mother and comfort her.

'Your sister is on the telephone,' said William, the next morning. 'Mother died early this morning,' said Donna. 'It was a heart attack.' Violet burst into tears and told her sister she would call her later.

'I should have stayed, William. I had no thought of her dying as she looked so fit except for the chest pain. You know how agile she has always been and never complained about any health problems.'

'She was 91 years old,' said William. 'She had no long illness and your sister was with her so maybe she was more fortunate than others who suffer years of treatment and pain.'

At the funeral in Devon Violet arranged for a recording of her piano music to be played. It was a sad and moving event for Violet and her sister, who managed to read an ideal poem. The flat had to be sold and personal items sorted but Donna was chief executor so she dealt with all the legal requirements.

'I think you need a trip to restore that happy smile I love,' said William. 'I have booked a flight to Nice so a few days in the south of France will help to soften the blow of losing your mother. She was such an amazing woman. Remember that time she went up those stairs in the restaurant at twice the speed of anyone else? She laughed when I failed to keep up with her. Just think of all the good times with her,' consoled William.

They enjoyed two weeks in Florida during the summer months and Violet joined her sailing friends for the annual trip to France. She had met Moira and Barry through the sailing club. They needed a crew member during the summer and Violet had offered her services. They sailed to France with another yacht that also had a married couple and a friend as crew. The six arrived in Cherbourg after a gentle Channel crossing and enjoyed some French cuisine at a local restaurant. Cooking for the evening meal was shared but there were favourite restaurants where Barry usually had moules mariniere and Moira indulged in a dish of oysters.

'Have you taken your seasickness pills?' asked Violet. 'No, I am trying the patches this time,' answered Moira.

'You should try the pills we used in America. They are called Bonnine and were originally designed to help cancer patients cope with nausea. They work for 24 hours and I found them really effective.'

The sailing schedule was from Cherbourg to the Channel Islands, then after several days relaxing in either Jersey or Guernsey they sailed back to the UK. Violet loved hoisting the spinnaker although Barry had organised the boat so that the sails could be managed from the cockpit. He called it the OAP yacht. Often Violet helmed while Barry was below deck plotting the course and Moira sat quietly feeling seasick.

Chapter 24

'I will be working over the Millennium New year, as there is a concern about the computers,' announced William. 'If they shut down the freight and passenger service will be disastrously affected.'

'Why will the computers shut down?' asked Violet. 'It is only another New Year.'

'Apparently computer systems' inability to distinguish dates correctly have the potential to bring down worldwide infrastructures for industries. That could be anything from banking to air travel,' replied William. 'It is being called the Millennium bug or Y2K.'

'Do we need to do anything? What about our Christmas arrangements? We have done all our food and presents shopping,' said Violet anxiously.

'Some experts argued that the coverage of the problem amounts to scaremongering and nothing serious will happen,' replied William. 'Places like Australia and countries in the Pacific will experience the change first so we will know before our New Year if there is a problem.'

'I will stay up and wait for you – into January 1st,' said Violet, laughing. William arrived home for a late breakfast in the New Year without any computer problems at the airport.

The pre-emptive action of many computer programmers and information technology experts had prevented any disaster.

January 2000 arrived with a surprising fall of snow. Violet took some photos and decided to plan a visit to a warm country for the spring half-term. 'There is a bouquet of flowers for you, Mrs Fullerton,' said the school secretary.

Violet opened the accompanying card and realised it was from William. Her birthday was soon so the words in the card were a complete surprise.

'Will you marry me, darling?'

William's proposal made Violet laugh out loud and the secretary, who had read the card, gave a big smile.

'I need to make a phone call. Can I use your office?'

'Of course you can,' replied the secretary. 'Take as long as you wish.' Violet rang his mobile as William was in his office at Heathrow airport.

'I will, I will,' said Violet excitedly. 'Why not a face to face proposal?'

'You might have refused,' said William, 'and this way it gave you time to consider. I was optimistic so booked a trip to Amsterdam for our engagement.'

'So you can buy me a really expensive diamond engagement ring. How thoughtful of you,' answered Violet with a smile.

His son and daughter were delighted and an engagement dinner was organised with family and friends.

Due to the possibility of Ward working abroad in the summer, the wedding date was arranged for the summer half-term. Violet chose a boat on the river for the ceremony with her favourite classical music being played as she walked down the aisle. William chose a big band recording at the end of the ceremony. The barge belonged to one of the Oxford Colleges and was moored outside a hotel on the Thames River. The floral arrangements inside were organised by Violet and the Registrar was delighted when she heard the ceremony was to be afloat. As Violet was an Aquarian she thought it totally apt. The honeymoon had to be only a week so Violet chose Valencia. They enjoyed the sunshine and sightseeing but Violet always made time for shopping. She had numerous fridge magnets from all the countries they had visited in addition to miniature souvenirs.

Although Valencia was extremely enjoyable Violet thought a longer honeymoon was necessary. She had always wanted to visit Hawaii so July saw them flying to Kauai for two weeks. It was an idyllic trip exceeding even Violet's expectations. On the flight home Violet felt her second marriage would be as successful as her marriage to Henry.

****

Epilogue

'Here's to twenty years of marriage, and hopefully to at least another decade,' said William, as he raised his champagne glass.

A celebration of their twenty years together had been arranged by Violet, preceded by a piano recital. She had given a performance for charity the day before and then invited numerous friends to a lunch. The recital had raised over one thousand pounds so the months of preparation had been worthwhile.

Everyone returned to Beechtree for tea and cake with more champagne. 'The time has passed so quickly,' said Violet to William. 'We have been enjoying so many activities and holidays since we both retired that the weeks have flown past. I miss the sailing and horse riding but I suppose age compels you to give up certain pleasures.'

'You still have the energy to perform piano recitals and the garden is spectacular again this year,' replied William.

'After all the excitement we can now have a quiet evening together watching a movie,' said Violet, giving William a loving kiss.

****

Ingram Content Group UK Ltd.
Milton Keynes UK
UKHW020638220623
423865UK00011B/588